Spider's Web

Sharon Stewart

Red Deer College Press

Northern Lights Young Novels are published by
Red Deer College Press
56 Avenue & 32 Street Box 5005
Red Deer Alberta Canada T4N 5H5

Acknowledgments
Edited for the Press by Peter Carver
Cover illustration by Kasio Charko
Cover design by Boldface Technologies Inc.
Printed and bound in Canada by WebCom for Red Deer College Press

Financial support provided by the Alberta Foundation for the Arts, a beneficiary of the Lottery Fund of the Government of Alberta, and by the Canada Council, the Department of Canadian Heritage and Red Deer College.

COMMITTED TO THE DEVELOPMENT OF CULTURE AND THE ARTS

THE CANADA COUNCIL | LE CONSEIL DES ARTS
FOR THE ARTS | DU CANADA
SINCE 1957 | DEPUIS 1957

Canadian Cataloguing in Publication
Stewart, Sharon (Sharon Roberta), 1944–
Spider's web
(Northern lights young novels)
ISBN 0-88995-177-2
I. Title. II. Series.
PS8587.T4895S64 1998   jC813'.54   C98-910247-5
PZ7.S852Sp 1998

5 4 3 2 1

To Roderick.
Always more reasons.

Chapter 1

Rich sunlight spilled through the windows of the city hall chapel as the minister's voice droned through the wedding service. Spider willed herself not to listen to the words he was saying. They were nothing she wanted to hear. Better to tune the whole scene out—she was good at that.

Phaser shields up! she told herself. No known energy in the universe can get through now!

She watched the minister's mouth opening and shutting. It worked! She couldn't hear a word.

But something else got through. A tapping sound caught her attention, and she looked around. A fly was beating itself against the glass of one of the long windows.

Trapped, you dummy, she thought. And nothing you can do about it.

She stood on one foot and gingerly rubbed the top of one yellow satin shoe against the back of her leg. The wretched shoes not only pinched, they made her feet look like Donald Duck's. In fact, she hated the whole fancy outfit her mother had insisted she must wear. It made her feel itchy all over. She glowered at her mother's back and then down at the bouquet of white orchids she had given her to hold during the service. The smell of them made her want to throw up. If her mother insisted on doing this, why did she, Spider, have to be dragged into it?

She'd made her feelings about the whole thing plain weeks ago, but it hadn't done any good.

"Of course you have to come, Sara," her mother had said. "I can't possibly get married without my daughter there."

"Why?"

"Because I love you, silly."

"Oh, yeah?"

Her mother's brows drew together. "Knock it off, Sara. We've gone over and over this. I thought I'd got you to understand how I feel."

"What about you understanding how *I* feel? Why should I have to watch my mother get married to a creep?" Spider asked.

"Why do you have to be so nasty about Andrew?" Joanna asked. "He isn't a creep, no matter what you think."

Spider scuffed a line in the pile of the carpet with the toe of her sneaker and said nothing. If there was one thing in the universe she was certain of, it was that Andrew Craven was a creep. Worse than that, he was a nerdy creep. A real supernerd.

And he didn't like her all that much either, Spider reflected. At least, he hardly ever said anything to her, just grinned at her in a dopey sort of way. She thought he looked relieved when she made excuses not to spend time with him and her mother.

Her mother waited for a moment, then said, "Do you honestly think I'd marry a creep?"

"Guess so, as long as he's rich enough. Andrew sure is that."

There, she'd said it. She'd been wanting to for a long time, and now she had. She wanted her mother to know how she had let herself and Spider down by getting involved with this guy. Sold out, that's what she'd done. And after all the years she'd talked about making it on her own. About how it was just the two of them, she and Spider, against the world.

Her mother's eyes widened with rage. Her hand flew up and for a minute Spider thought she was going to slap her. Though she never had in her whole life. Not ever.

And didn't now. Her mother turned pale. Her hand dropped, and the two of them stood glaring at each other.

"All right," her mother said at last. "You've had your say—and it was a rotten thing to say, too. Now you're going to listen." She drew a deep breath. "You'll come to the wedding, and you'll behave yourself. And I won't listen to another word about it. Do you understand?" She held her daughter's gaze until Spider dropped her eyes.

"Yes . . . *Joanna*," Spider mumbled. She knew that would hurt. Well, too bad. If it wasn't enough for her mother to be her mother, if she wanted to be some guy's wife instead, why should she call her "Mom"?

That had been the end of it, and now it was too late.

". . . pronounce you man and wife."

Somehow, the words sneaked through Spider's phaser shield and zapped her back into focus. The thing was done, and there was nothing to do but watch miserably as Andrew Craven kissed his bride. Supernerd, who usually looked as if he were plugged in somewhere else, was actually beaming. And her mother looked as if someone had lit a candle inside her, Spider thought, swallowing a lump in her throat.

The wedding photographer, who had been lurking discreetly in the background, stepped forward and took a few quick pictures of the bride and groom. Then Joanna beckoned Spider and Carter Craven, Andrew's son by his first marriage, to join them, and the camera clicked away again. After a few more shots, Andrew impatiently waved the photographer away, and the man backed off at once.

At least that's over, thought Spider, who hated having her picture taken. She blinked, trying to get rid of the blue flashes in front of her eyes.

Carter Craven went over to his father and shook his

hand. Spider, who had never seen him before the ceremony, had sneaked a couple of peeks at him before the service. Blond and blue-eyed, he looked like someone that belonged on the cover of a fan 'zine.

Must get his looks from his mother, thought Spider, narrowing her eyes and glancing from Carter to his father and back. He sure doesn't look like Supernerd. Which was just as well. She didn't like anything about Andrew Craven—not his nerdiness and not his money. But she really hated the way he looked, especially now, standing next to her beautiful mother. He was short and skinny with lank brown hair that flopped over his forehead. And he wore glasses, thick ones, that always looked as though they needed cleaning.

"Way to go, Dad," said Carter smoothly. "Congratulations, Joanna." He kissed Spider's mother on the cheek.

Smooth creep, son of nerdy creep, thought Spider. She was willing to bet that Carter was no more thrilled about the wedding than she was, but he wasn't about to let his father see it. Knew which side his bread was buttered on probably. All those Craven millions. Or was it billions? Gazillions?

"Sara?" said her mother, reaching out to her. Spider let herself be kissed. She even squeezed her eyes shut and let Supernerd kiss her cheek. No one could say she wasn't cooperating. But she scowled at Carter. There was no way she was going to let *him* kiss her!

Luckily, he didn't try. Spider could feel him looking her over. He looked a bit puzzled, she thought. Like a kid who got the wrong prize out of the cereal box. He probably thought she looked pretty weird. Not the kind of daughter her mother should have. She glared at him.

When Joanna and Andrew went to sign the register, Carter came over and pumped Spider's hand up and down. "Well, Sis, guess we're just one happy family now," he said. His voice had an edge to it that put Spider on her guard, and his eyes were cold. He didn't mean a word of it. What a phony!

"Yeah, sure," Spider muttered, still frowning. "Just don't call me 'Sis'."

Carter raised his eyebrows. "Cool by me, Bugface," he shot back. "I prefer human relatives anyway."

Spider flushed, making the small, purple, spider-shaped mark stand out even more vividly on her cheek.

"Carter! For shame!" This from the tall, dark-haired woman who was a witness at the ceremony. All Spider knew about her was that her name was Margarita Par, and she worked for Andrew Craven.

Supernerd must pay her plenty, Spider reflected, taking in her outfit. The woman looked sleek and cool from the top of her shining cap of hair to the soles of her expensive-looking shoes.

"Sorry, Mia," said Carter, grinning. He didn't look even a little abashed. "Guess my evil nature just gets the better of me sometimes." He strolled after the bridal couple, his hands in his pockets.

"I'm afraid Carter takes some getting used to, Sara," the woman said, turning to Spider with a rueful smile. "Sometimes he can be pure vinegar—I should know. Just don't let him get your goat, no matter how hard he tries."

"He won't," promised Spider.

Just then, Andrew put his head around the door of the registry. "Come on, Mia, you're our other witness. We need your signature or the whole thing isn't legal," he said.

"Can't have that," said Mia with a quick smile. She hurried into the registry.

Spider turned back into the chapel. The fly was still beating its brains out against the glass.

"C'mon, stupid, this is your lucky day," said Spider. She cupped her hand behind the fly and snatched. Then she shook her closed fist, gloating for a moment at the tickle of frantic wings. After a moment she carried it outside to the steps of the city hall and let it go.

What could be taking them so long? Spider felt silly standing around in her fancy dress, still holding the dumb flowers. She scuffed her way down the steps, taking care to graze the heels of her satin shoes against the concrete. No way she'd ever have to wear them again.

At the bottom, a blimp-sized, white limousine idled, waiting to take Andrew and her mother to the airport. Seeing her, the driver, a friendly-looking man with a black handlebar mustache, got out. "Nice day for a wedding, Miss," he said, grinning, as he opened the car doors.

Spider ignored him.

Joanna and Andrew appeared with Carter and Mia behind them.

"I can't believe we actually got away with it without the press finding out," Andrew gloated. "I was expecting a real scrum."

"Especially with your pictures splashed all over the paper when you two got engaged," added Mia. "I say it's a lucky omen!"

Andrew turned and kissed her on the cheek. "Thanks for the good vibes, lady," he joked. Then he tried to kiss Spider's cheek again. Deciding that one kiss in a day was more than enough, she ducked, and he got the top of her head instead.

"C'mon, Missus," he said, turning to Joanna. "If we don't move it we're going to miss that plane."

Joanna hugged Spider, who stood numbly on the curb, still clutching the bouquet. Then she and Andrew got into the car. Joanna lowered the window, beckoning to Spider. "I do understand how you feel, hon," she said in a low voice. "Thanks for being a good sport. Believe me, everything will work out okay."

Good sport! Spider was outraged. "Sure . . . *Joanna*," she snapped.

The window whined up and the car purred away.

A trash can stood nearby, and with one deft flip Spider sent the white orchids sailing into it. A perfect basket.

Chapter 2

The Craven place sat way back from the road, screened by a grove of tall pines. Spider squirmed in the front seat of Carter's low-slung, foreign sports car, craning her neck to get a glimpse of her new home. Mia had told Carter to drive Spider over.

"You two might as well get used to each other," she'd said. Carter opened his mouth to protest, but she gave him a quelling look.

Who was Mia trying to kid? thought Spider. They'd hated each other on sight, hadn't they? Sure enough, the only words they'd exchanged the whole way was about his car.

Mucho weirdo, Spider had thought when Carter picked her up in it. The car looked sort of like a squashed soap dish on wheels.

"What *is* this thing?" she asked.

Carter raised his eyebrows. "It's a Porsche," he said, his tone of voice showing what he thought of people too dumb to know that.

"Oh," said Spider. Even the name was weird, she thought. Like someone making a rude noise. She decided that it suited Carter pretty well.

Now the car turned between two stone pillars and swept

11

up a curving gravel drive. The car crunched to a halt, and Spider stared around her. Where was the house?

"This is *it?*" The question popped out before she could stop herself. She'd been expecting something totally different—a mansion, for sure. Maybe even a château with turrets, like the Fantasyland castle at Disney World. But certainly not just a long stone wall with a single massive door set into it.

"Yep." Carter shot her a mocking glance. "Surprised?"

Spider shrugged. She'd never admit it.

Carter hoisted himself over the side of the car, and after a small struggle with the door handle, Spider clambered awkwardly out.

Mia, who had gone on ahead of them, was already opening the door. She pressed her palm flat against a panel set into the wall. A light flashed and the door swung open. She smiled at Spider as she came up and waved her through. "Welcome to your new home, Sara," she said.

Spider stuck out her chin and stalked past her. This would never be home. Home was the apartment she and her mother had lived in for years. Cozy and sunny and just big enough for two.

She stopped dead, staring. Whatever this house was, it wasn't cozy. It was glowing wood and stone and light and the murmur of water. She found herself standing at the top of a steep ravine, with the whole house dropping away in levels below her. Down, down, down it went, until the bottom floor blended into the dusk. There were windows everywhere, looking out into trees on two sides. On the third, a wall of glass revealed a stream that emerged from under one wing of the house and ran along a shallow stone channel before plunging down into the ravine below.

"The house is called Fallingbrook, Sara," said Mia. "I hope you'll be happy here."

Spider said nothing. If they thought she'd act impressed and *ooh* and *ah* they had the wrong person.

"Your mother loves it," Mia added.

I bet she does, thought Spider grimly and made up her mind to hate it.

Almost as if the house had read her mind, a breath of cool air fanned her hot cheek. Soft lights began to come on in the gathering dusk, and floodlights picked out the gleam of the waterfall as it leaped down into the ravine.

Mia was going on about the house. "It's a pretty unusual place, you know. Not just the way it looks, either. In a way, it's Andrew's personal toy. He and his engineers have figured out every possible way computers could be used to operate a house." She grinned. "Sometimes you'd almost swear the place is alive."

Carter pretended to stifle a yawn. "Oh, lord, it's the *Better Homes and Gardens* tour! Sorry, it always affects me like this." He turned toward the door.

"Now, why don't you stay and have supper with us?" asked Mia. "It's all laid on for us—cold lobster, the works."

Yechhh! thought Spider. Lobsters always reminded her of big, dead bugs. Cold ones didn't bear thinking about.

"Not for me, thanks. Have to head back to the frat house. Lots of heavy studying to do." Carter winked at Spider, who stared back coldly.

"I bet," said Mia. "Beer and pool, more likely. Or worse."

"Who, me? Now is that a nice thing to say in front of Bugface?"

Mia's expression became stony. "If I hear that word come out of your mouth one more time, I'll stop your allowance. Don't think I can't do it, either."

"Oh, I believe you. Dad eats out of your hand. Or used to. Why, I'm surprised he even dared to get married. Or did he ask your permission first?"

"That's enough, Carter!" snapped Mia.

Carter grinned, clearly pleased at her reaction. "It is, isn't it? Well, don't worry. Now that Dad's away, there's no reason for me to hang around the place. No Boy Scout points in it. So I'll catch you later, Mia. Much later. You, too, B . . . Sis." The door slammed behind him.

Mia rolled her eyes. "Andrew keeps hoping that boy will straighten out, but there's no sign of it. That awful mother of his must let him get away with murder." She sighed, then added, "Sorry, Sara. This isn't much of an introduction to your new family."

Spider shrugged. "That's okay," she said. "I wasn't expecting much."

Mia looked at her hard for a moment, then her expression softened. "Poor kid, you must be worn out. Let me show you your room first. We can worry about food later."

"I'm not hungry. Weddings make me barfy," mumbled Spider. There was no way she was going to face one of those lobsters. She'd starve first!

Reluctantly, she followed Mia down an open stairway and off to the left. As they walked along, recessed ceiling lights came on ahead of them, casting pools of light on the polished floor.

"The house computer has motion and heat detectors," explained Mia. "It knows when you enter and leave a room, and adjusts the lighting."

"What if you like the dark?" asked Spider, who didn't, much.

"There are remote controls that can override the default settings," said Mia. "I'll show you all that later. Now, this is your room," she added, opening a door at the end of the passage. "All your things are still packed up, I'm afraid."

A good thing, too, thought Spider. She hated anyone messing with her stuff.

Mia stepped across to a panel set into the wall and pressed a switch. "You can see why we call this room the Treehouse," she went on, as the drapes whispered back into recesses in the wall.

Spider found herself among treetops looking south and west through floor-to-ceiling windows on two sides. One wall of glass was actually a set of sliding doors that gave onto a small deck right amongst the trees. Drawn despite herself, she went over. The doors opened smoothly ahead of her, and she stepped out into the dusk and the whisper of falling water.

Well, hairy bananas! Spider said to herself. So this is how rich people live. But she was careful to keep her face blank as she stepped back into the room. No way she was going to look impressed or anything.

"Your closets and bathroom are over here, Sara," said Mia, opening a door. "And this is a special present for you from Andrew." She pressed another control switch and a panel on one wall slid away, revealing a work station with an elaborate computer setup. The screen was enormous.

"Didn't Mom—I mean, Joanna—tell you I'm not interested in that stuff?"

"She did, actually. But Andrew thought . . . Well, you never know. You must need to use a computer for your homework sometimes."

"I can use the ones at school, thanks." Although she almost never did. Computers were her mother's world, and she wanted no part of it.

"Well, here it is, anyway. Andrew left a message for you in your e-mail box."

Spider said nothing, wishing that Mia would go away and leave her alone.

Right on cue, Mia said, "I'll leave you on your own to settle in now."

She must have ESP, thought Spider.

"I'll put all the food in the fridge in case you decide you're hungry after all. It's easy to find the kitchen—just keep going downhill." She pointed to a phone beside the computer. "I'll be here if you want me. Just call—my house extension is MP." She went out, closing the door behind her.

Spider thumped down on the low bed and kicked off her Donald Duck shoes. Well, here she was. Stuck. Her pile of possessions looked small and shabby huddled in one corner of the room.

She wished now that she had agreed to move in sooner, as her mother had wanted.

15

"It'll be awful for you if we don't move to Fallingbrook until after the wedding," Joanna had fretted. "We could make the move sooner, together, and then you'd be all settled in by the time Andrew and I go away."

"I'd rather stay here as long I can," Spider had insisted. "After all, it's my home. It isn't too much to ask, is it?"

Joanna had sighed. "Of course it isn't. But . . . oh, well, have it your way."

And she had. But that wasn't much comfort now, with her mother gone and her belongings in boxes all around her. Tears welled up in Spider's eyes. She felt as if she could cry a puddle, a pool, a lake of them. Fill up the world until she drowned. But what good would tears do? She gave a huge sniff and fought them back. Darn Andrew Craven and his money, anyway, she thought. Everything had been great until he came along.

Oh? asked a small voice deep inside her. She squelched it, relishing her anger. Her mother was her mother. She was too old to get married again. It was disgusting, and she'd told her so. Not that it had done any good.

To her indignation, Joanna had just laughed. Great hoots of laughter.

"Sara, I know I seem as old as Methuselah to you. But I'm not ready for the boneyard yet!"

"I didn't say that!" Spider had snapped. "And I don't see what's so funny."

Seeing how angry she was, her mother had stopped laughing. "I'm only thirty-five, Sara," she said. "I was very young when I married your father, and I had you just a few years after. Then when he . . . died, things were so hard for so long. You're too young to remember the worst of it."

"But it's not like that now!" Spider protested.

"No, it's not. I've got you and a great job, and things are so much easier," her mother replied. "But there's still something missing. Someone my own age to share my life with. Pretty soon you'll be all grown up. Going to university, moving out. You won't want a clinging-vine mother

16

hanging around your neck then. And you shouldn't!"

"How do you know what I want?"

Joanna had got up and tried to put her arm around her, but Spider moved away. "Can't you trust me a little, Sara?" she asked. "I wouldn't do anything I thought would hurt you, even if it was something I wanted really badly. You know that."

"You've always said we decide everything together," accused Spider. "Now you won't listen to me. It's not fair! You love him better than me!"

Joanna reached out and smoothed Spider's long bangs out of her eyes. "Now you're being childish, and you know it," she said. She sighed. "You're right in one way, though. I did say we'd decide everything together. And I was wrong. This is one thing I have to decide for both of us."

She'd decided, all right, thought Spider. Rotten Andrew Craven had won. Now here she was, stuck in his wired-up morgue of a house. And he was off around the world with her mother. For a whole month.

And he'd left her a stupid message. Spider sighed and got up. Might as well get it over with. Mia would probably bug her until she did. She had already figured out that Mia was the bugging type. She went over to the computer and pressed the power switch.

There was a soft *ping*, and the screen lit up. For a moment, colors swirled, then a voice said, "Hi, Sara, what can I do for you?"

"Yikes!" yelped Spider, whirling around. But there was no one behind her. When she looked back at the screen, though, an image had appeared. It was a stylized picture of a crouching cat with pointed ears and long whiskers. It wore a most peculiar grin that annoyed Spider on sight, as if it reminded her of something she couldn't quite remember.

"What's your pleasure?" it asked. "I do word processing, games, graphics, telecommunications, and lots more. See for yourself." The Cat vanished and a menu with picture icons appeared. It read:

GameCat
ArtCat
WordCat
TelCat
MailCat
HouseCat

"Well, mail must be in MailCat," she muttered and clicked the mouse on the icon.

The Cat reappeared. "Mail coming up," it said. It shrank to a small icon at one side of the screen while the mail menu appeared. Then the image of a white rabbit in a waist-coat and jacket, holding a large pocket watch in its paws, popped out of the side of the menu. The hands raced around the watch face, then the rabbit pulled a trumpet out of its pocket and blew it.

"Ta-da! You have in-house mail, Sara," the Cat remarked, grinning. "Want to read it? Just say yes or click on Read Mail."

"Yes?" said Sara. She couldn't believe this was happening to her. Whoever heard of a talking computer?

A message flashed up on the screen:

From: andrew@cravencomp.com
To: sara
Subject: welcome
Hi, Sara:

Hope you like my little surprise. Joanna says you hate all this stuff, but—who knows?—it may grow on you. You are your mother's daughter, after all.

What I really wanted to say to you, though, is that I hope you can get used to having me around. Your mother and I love each other, but there's not just us to think about, is there?

I know we haven't hit it off all that well up to now, Sara. I've got a pretty good idea of what you think of my barging into your life

18

and changing everything. I wish I could say I'm sorry, but I can't. Meeting your mom was the best thing that ever happened to me. For some reason she seems to feel the same about me. And we both want you to be a part of it. Maybe it won't be easy, but can we at least give it a try?
See you soon.

Andrew

Creep, thought Spider. Does he think he can bribe me into liking him? He may have bought my mother, but he can't buy me!

Angrily, she punched the power switch to turn the computer off. She knew just enough about computers to know you weren't supposed to do that in the middle of a program, but she was feeling vindictive.

The computer beeped loudly, but stayed on.

"Ow!" said the Cat, which had enlarged again. "Don't *do* that! It scrambles my brains. Just say 'quit' to turn me off."

"Oh, shut up!" snarled Spider.

But the Cat just stayed there, grinning. "Say it nicely," it insisted.

"All right, all right. Quit!" she ordered.

"Catch you later, Sara," said the Cat. It winked, then pixel by pixel, it slowly disappeared, leaving its grin behind it. In a moment that too faded and the screen went blank.

> > >

It was late when he got off the plane from Toronto. Lucky he didn't have to hang around waiting for baggage, he told himself, swinging his solitary duffel bag.

He flagged a cab and settled in for the ride downtown. Feeling around in an inner pocket of his windbreaker, he pulled out a folded newspaper clipping and read the headline again by the glare of the streetlights.

"Computer Billionaire Andrew Craven to Wed Employee," it read. He stared down at the two faces frozen in the grainy black and white photo, reliving his feelings when he'd first seen it in the paper. The shock. Then the rising tide of bitterness. Some guy must have got that one with a telephoto lens, he told himself now. Craven was famous for being camera-shy, and he'd be willing to bet the bride-to-be was, too. From the look on her face.

He checked his watch. After 1:00 A.M. Yesterday was the day. He'd seen a headline about the wedding in the evening paper. They'd be married by now, and off on—how did the paper report it?—their whirlwind global honeymoon. For a month or so. Plenty of time to find out what he needed to know and even the score.

But first things first. He'd need a place to stay. And then a job. And he knew exactly where he could get one.

Chapter 3

Mia put down *The Wall Street Journal* and peered at Spider over the tops of her half-moon glasses. "Are you *sure* that's what you usually wear to school?" she asked warily, taking in Spider's ripped jeans and man-sized plaid shirt with the tail hanging out.

"Sure I'm sure," said Spider, downing her orange juice.

"Funny," said Mia. "Back in the Stone Age when I was a teenager, girls took a lot of trouble to look like girls."

Spider shrugged.

"Anyway, move it. You're going to be late for school!" Mia went on. "At least eat your toast while I get the car out."

Spider made a face as soon as Mia's back was turned. Why should she care what Spider wore or whether or not she was late? She settled her baseball cap on backward, slung her backpack over her shoulder, and trudged upstairs.

I wonder why Supernerd hasn't put in an escalator, she thought. This was worse than climbing the Himalayas, and you have to do it umpteen times a day!

Mia was waiting behind the wheel of an expensive-looking, silver-grey car. Spider thumped in beside her and sniffed loudly. The car smelled of new leather. She rubbed her hand against the seat. It was buttery-soft. She peered at the logo on the dash. Mercedes, it read. Another weirdo name.

"Cool car Andrew has," she said, as it pulled smoothly away. Then she added, "But I was kind of expecting a uniformed chauffeur and all, you know?"

"Sorry to disappoint you," replied Mia. "None of us is all that decrepit. We actually still manage to drive ourselves around."

We? wondered Spider. This woman talked as though she were one of the family.

"And this isn't Andrew's car, by the way," Mia added. "It's mine."

"It's *your* car?" Spider asked, puzzled.

Mia shot her a sidelong glance. "Oh, yes," she purred. "Back in Manila I used to drive this real cute little donkey cart, but somehow it just didn't do here on the freeway. So I have to put up with this. Tough, huh?"

Hoo boy, thought Spider and lapsed into glum silence for the rest of the trip.

Mia dropped her off in front of Riverside High. "I'll pick you up after three," she said. "Unless you want to hang out with your friends."

"Don't have any," mumbled Spider.

Mia shrugged. "Okay. See you later then."

Spider got out, slamming the car door harder than necessary. She shouldered her backpack and tramped grimly into the building, feeling her school self close around her. It might, just might, have been worth it for her mother to get married if it had got her out of her old school. But no. Here she was, stuck in the same old place. Just her luck. The smell of the hallways made her queasy. She'd felt that way ever since she had arrived in grade seven.

She was late, of course. Her stomach clenched. She hadn't eaten breakfast, and now she felt kind of sick and giddy. She had Mr. Batsford's English class first, too, just to make things really gruesome. It didn't help that the Bat was her homeroom teacher. She knew what he'd say: "Well, if it isn't the late Sara Weber." That's what he always said when she was late. Which was often.

She opened the door cautiously, but, to her surprise, a strange teacher was in front of the class. Hey, a substitute, she thought, pleased. Things were looking up.

"I'm sorry I'm late," she mumbled. "We moved, and . . ."

The substitute was a young guy who already looked frazzled. She could tell by the look of him that he'd be hamburger by lunchtime. "Okay, okay, just sit down. What's your name?" he asked, flipping open the attendance book.

"Sara Weber."

He checked her name off. "Okay, Sara. You're in. But take that cap off in class."

A couple of girls giggled. Spider ignored them.

"Yo, Spider," one of the boys muttered as she edged past him to get to her desk. "How does it feel be the daughter of Daddy Megabucks?"

"Funny, she doesn't look any different," Lauren Pringle snickered, tossing her sleek blonde hair. "Guess money can't buy everything."

It figured that Lauren would get in the knife, thought Spider. Girls who didn't try to look like Barbie dolls seemed to get right up Lauren's nose. Maybe they reminded her there were other life-forms on the planet. Then Spider tripped over a foot Greg Harris, the class clown, had stuck out into the aisle. She landed on her knees, her backpack spilling paper and books onto the floor.

"Oops," said Greg, grinning.

Spider stared up at him. What was it with him, anyway? She knew he had done it on purpose. He was always on her case, with his goons behind him. Like a bunch of wolves who knew they could pick off a dumb, slow deer that lagged behind the herd.

A lot of kids thought Greg was a real funny guy, but Spider noticed his jokes always had victims, and when he went after them, his eyes got all hot and shiny. Almost, Spider thought, as though he needed to be mean to get a kind of power he couldn't get any other way. It spooked her to even think about him. It was easier to see people as kind of simple. Sort of two-dimensional, like playing cards.

All she could do was to try to ignore Greg, but it never worked. He always knew he was getting to her. He could feel it, smell her fear.

"Maaan, she is sooo clumsy," one of Greg's buddies chimed in.

More snickers all around.

Knees throbbing, Spider began picking up books and papers and stuffing them into her bag. Jerry Conway, who sat behind her, reached down and handed her some. He rolled his eyes at her, then looked away.

How much lower can I get? wondered Spider. Even a geek like Jerry Conway gets embarrassed looking at me!

Trying to ignore the pain in her knees, she sat down at her desk. She slouched down and pulled off her cap, letting her lank hair fall around her face like curtains. She could imagine them all grinning. She might as well have a neon label across her forehead: Weird Spider Weber—Misfit and Social Reject.

It was going to be a great day. She could tell.

Mia picked her up just after 3:15. A bunch of guys, Greg Harris among them, stood smoking just outside school property. When the sleek, grey car pulled up, cheers and cat-calls broke out.

"Yeeee-hah! Look at that set of wheels!"

"Hey, Cinderella," Greg yelled, "can I have a ride in your carriage? Oh, pleeeeeze!" He fell on one knee in mock pleading, his hand over his heart.

It doesn't matter what I do, thought Spider. When I'm just a dumb klutz they go for me. Now that I'm riding around in a fancy car, they go for me, too.

"Cute bunch," commented Mia as Spider got in. "How was your day?"

"Terrific," said Spider.

"I suppose they all knew about the wedding. Andrew tried to keep it out of the papers, but I saw a front-page story this morning."

"They knew all right." It was funny, Spider reflected. Most of the kids had teased her about it, but a few had acted impressed. As though Andrew's money had anything to do with her!

"Never mind. They'll lose interest after a while and forget all about it."

"Yeah, sure." The trouble was, she couldn't. For the rest of her life she'd have nerdy Andrew Craven and Craven Computers International hung around her neck.

Mia gave her a sideways glance and said, "You'll get used to it all, you know."

Spider said nothing. Darn Mia's ESP, anyway. It was beginning to make her edgy.

"I know you haven't got to know Andrew all that well," Mia went on. "You probably think he's a bit odd. Most people do. But he's really a great guy. Shy, though. I can tell you he's a lot easier to get along with since he met your mother. Seems happier than he's ever been."

Swell, thought Spider. She figured she'd better not say it aloud. This Mia was no softy. Except maybe where Andrew Craven was concerned.

"And, you know," Mia went on, "it's not just Joanna. I suspect that deep down Andrew is thrilled at the idea of having a daughter now. It's a whole different thing from having a son, after all."

Oh, gag, thought Spider. No wonder he wanted a daughter. Anyone who had a son like Carter would want to give something else a try! Well, if Supernerd wanted a sweetie-poo daughter he should have had one of his own before now. He'd soon find out that she wasn't going to fill the role! "Uh, how come you know so much about Andrew?" she asked, trying to sound casual. "Have you known him a long time?"

"Oh, practically forever. My mother worked for his parents. He and I grew up together, in a kind of way. When I finished my MBA degree, he asked me to work for him."

"I thought you used to drive a donkey cart in Manila," said Spider slyly.

Mia tucked a shiny wing of hair behind one ear and grinned. "Oh, that was just jive. You jive me, I jive you. Get it?"

Spider said nothing for a moment, then, "What about Carter?"

"What about him?"

"Does he live with Andrew? With . . . us?"

Mia rolled her eyes. "Not really. When it suits him, and that's not too often. He mostly lives at his frat house during the university year. Summers and holidays he usually spends with DeeDee. That's his mother, Andrew's ex-wife. Though she's remarried and doesn't have a lot of time for him. Too busy buying yachts for her new husband."

"I didn't know servants were supposed to talk like that." The words popped out before Spider realized she was speaking aloud.

Mia geared down for a stoplight. "You're an expert on servants?"

"No," faltered Spider. "But I thought . . . because you're looking after me—feeding me, driving me around . . ."

Mia gave her a level look. "Let's get one thing straight right from the start, Sara. I am not a servant. Not Andrew Craven's and certainly not yours. I'm Andrew's employee, just as your mother is at Craven International. Except that I run the estate and a whole lot of other private business holdings. I don't live at Fallingbrook, and I don't work there, either. My office is downtown in the Craven Tower. Right at the top."

She paused, as if to make sure that her words had registered, then went on, "As a friend of Andrew's, I've agreed to stay with you at the house while he and your mother are away. While I'm here, I'll make sure you get to school and back every day. Joanna and Andrew both think that's a good idea. And I'll see to our meals. But I won't be cleaning up after you or making your bed or doing your laundry."

The light turned green, and Mia stepped on the accelerator, whooshing Spider back into the expensive upholstery.

"Then who will?" asked Spider, surprised.

"Who has always done those things for you?"

"Well, sometimes M . . . I mean, Joanna. Mostly me."

"Then that's who will still do them."

"But . . . I thought Andrew was rich!"

"He is. Incredibly."

"So why doesn't he pay people to do stuff for him?" Spider demanded. "I would!"

Mia chuckled. "Guess he's just peculiar that way. Actually, Andrew doesn't really spend a lot of time at Fallingbrook—or hasn't until now."

She swung the big car off Riverside Drive and onto the road that led to the house. "He has an apartment in the Craven Tower," she went on. "He stays there all week. Eats there, too. So he's mostly at Fallingbrook only on weekends, and then he prefers to be on his own or just invite a few friends. Oh, there's a cleaning service that comes in to keep the place tidy. But you won't find any servants at Fallingbrook."

Jeez! thought Spider. What's the fun of being rich if you just live like everybody else?

Fallingbrook wasn't "living like everybody else," though. Mia had had her scan her palm print into the house computer's memory that morning. Now, when Spider got out of the car and pressed her palm against the entry panel, the door swung open. As if the house really knows I'm here, she thought. Maybe it does, with all those invisible security cameras and electric eyes.

It made her uncomfortable just thinking about it. Spider slunk down the hall to her room, cowed by the light and space around her. The Treehouse at least felt a little more comfortable, especially with all her stuff lying around. She began putting put some of it away, then stopped, alarmed at the way her things disappeared into built-in drawers and closets. If she wasn't careful, no one would even know she lived here.

She decided to fix that. She got out her biggest and loudest posters and taped them to the walls with masking tape. She even taped some on the windows. She put her favorite Star Trek TNG one across from her bed and stood for a moment gazing deeply into Captain Picard's eyes. He was so incredibly cool. Dignified in a sexy sort of way. Pretty old, though. Spider couldn't remember her father, and her mother had only a couple of old, blurred snapshots of him that didn't tell her much. But she thought—hoped—that he might have been something like Picard. Wise. Laid back. The kind of person you could tell your troubles to.

She kicked her shoes under the bed and dumped the rest of her clothes onto chairs or on the floor. The suitcases she stowed away in the closets.

That's more like it, she told herself, pleased. You could see that she lived here now. Definitely.

The only thing that was still un-Spider was the dweeb painting over the bed. It was of a girl wearing a fussy dress and an incredibly ugly hat that looked like an upside-down flowerpot. She was holding a limp rose. Spider leaned closer, trying to see how the painting was hung and whether she could take it down. The artist's signature was scribbled across one corner, just like a Roots label. It was a pretty terrible scrawl. R . . . something. Renoir? Then she realized it wasn't a painting at all. It was a flat computer screen with the image of the painting on it.

Spider groaned. Was *everything* in this house done with computers?

Anyway, there was clearly no way to get the darn thing off the wall. Too bad she was out of posters. She could have papered it over.

She tossed her backpack on the desk and got out her homework. There was a ton of it, as usual. She sighed and pulled out her French and Spanish texts. She was still wrestling with irregular verbs when Mia phoned to call her to supper.

"Can I watch TV while I eat?" Spider asked, looking around the kitchen for a set.

"Sure. That's just one of the things I haven't shown you yet." Mia picked up a computer remote from the counter and punched some keys. The large "painting" on one wall suddenly flickered and disappeared. A moment later the logo of a familiar channel sprang up.

Mia handed her the remote. "Just press the numbers at the bottom to change channels," she said. "Or you can pre-program it to catch your favorite shows every week. Or record them, like a VCR. Or order selections from a pay channel."

"What are those?" Spider eyed a row of colored symbols and buttons at the top of the remote.

"House settings. Remember I said you could change things around to suit you? You can change the air conditioning, set the alarms, pre-program the stove. And tons more stuff. Even an emergency generator."

"Yeah, but what's the symbol?"

Mia grinned. "A cat. His HouseCat, Andrew calls it."

Spider peered at the buttons. Sure enough, each bore the outline of a crouching cat, tail curled neatly around its paws. "Got it," she said. "It runs my computer, too."

"See this little touch screen set into the wall? They're all over the house. You can call up the house controls on a screen by pressing a button on the remote—blue cat for air conditioning, red cat for heat, and so on. Then you adjust the settings by touching the screen. Here, let me show you."

Mia pressed a key on the remote. A layout map of one floor of the house appeared on the screen. "That's a temperature map. You can see some rooms are cooler than others. If you want to change the temperature where you are, you just touch the screen. See? I've just increased the kitchen temperature by two degrees."

Spider reached over. "So if I touch the screen twice here, the temperature goes down again."

"Right." Mia pressed the remote again and the touch screen faded to silver. "There's more," she went on. "See that small grating in the wall, where the red light is? That's what Andrew calls a Cat's Ear. They're located all over the house. You can use them to do all the same commands by voice alone. But it's trickier, so people usually don't bother." She turned toward the grating and in a slow, robotlike voice said, "HouseCat. Kitchen. Video. Off."

Instantly, the TV image on the big screen dissolved into the abstract "painting" Spider had seen before.

"See what I mean?" asked Mia. "Keying it in is easier."

"Hold it, Cat," said Spider loudly, "turn that TV back on!"

"Oh, you can't just talk to it normally," Mia began, "You have to . . ." Her words died away as the TV quietly turned itself back on.

"Looks like *I* can," said Spider, feeling oddly smug.

Mia shook her head, smiling. "Amazing. Andrew was fiddling around a lot with the house systems before the wedding. He didn't tell me he'd modified HouseCat. It must have been part of what he was doing with your computer."

Spider scowled. "Some nerve he has, using my voice like that!" she said. "He must have taped me sometime."

"If you only knew what it means!" Mia said quickly. "This must be one of the first natural speech recognition systems on the planet. And he's programmed it to respond only to you. Don't you think it's a great present?"

Spider shrugged. Well, let's not get all dewy-eyed, she thought.

Spider watched TV until Mia looked at the clock and asked for the fourth time if she was absolutely sure all her homework was done. Obviously, the woman thought she had to act like some kind of watchdog. What a drag! Spider wandered back to her room. She had math to do, but somehow she couldn't get into it the way she usually did. She also had an English paper to write for the Bat, one he had assigned last week. She didn't even want to think about that. No matter what she did for him it wouldn't be good enough anyway. He was always on her case to try harder. If there was one thing she couldn't stand, it was teachers who thought she had a potential to live up to!

She threw down her pencil and wandered out onto the deck. It was quiet except for the sound of the water tumbling into the ravine. Spooky. Almost like not being in a city at all.

She glanced at the computer, then away. The Cat was weird, all right, but . . .

She booted up the computer. The screen filled with colors again, and then the Cat appeared and asked her what she wanted. Spider scanned the menu. Most of it was easy to figure out now that she knew more about it. HouseCat must give her the same house controls as the remote in the kitchen.

That gave her an idea. "HouseCat," she said loudly. Instantly, a control panel identical to the one she had seen on the screen downstairs appeared. Spider eyed it for a moment. The climate controls and lights were obvious, but she couldn't see how . . .

"Uh, Cat? How can I change the painting in my room?" she asked.

The Cat reappeared. "You don't like the Renoir?" it inquired.

"No," said Spider.

"But it was specially chosen for you."

By Supernerd, of course. Probably his warped idea of what girls liked. What did *he* know? "No!" she repeated.

"Well, then, what *do* you want? Craven International holds the computer display rights to most of the world's finest art."

"Got any hot rock posters?" asked Spider.

"Posters of hot rocks?" The Cat sounded puzzled.

"No, dummy. Rock groups—musicians," said Spider.

There was a brief pause, and then the Cat replied. "Nothing like that in my archive."

"Oh, poop. Well then, pick something else that you *do* have."

The Renoir winked out and another portrait appeared in its place. Spider had seen this one before. It was a woman called Mona-something. Her smile was even more annoying than the Cat's grin.

"No," said Spider.

Next she got a Madonna with angels.

"No!"

An abstract painting that made her cross-eyed just looking at it.

"Gimme a break!"

"Picky, aren't you?" complained the Cat, as a cartoon image of Porky Pig flashed up on the wall.

"Very funny. No! Give me something that looks like something real, for cripes' sake."

"Why didn't you say so?" asked the Cat. Porky Pig winked out and a giant tin of tomato soup popped up.

"*That's* a painting?" asked Spider.

"A very famous one," said the Cat primly. "By Andy Warhol."

Spider cocked her head, considering. It was radical. "I kind of like it," she admitted after a moment. "At least I know what I'm looking at."

"Hooray!" said the Cat. On the computer screen, the main menu reappeared.

Spider scanned it again. TelCat. What on Earth was that? Some fancy kind of telephone? Only one way to find out.

"TelCat!" she said loudly.

"It's about time," the Cat remarked and disappeared.

The screen turned blue, then green, and the cat logo appeared. Letters flashed up underneath it.

Welcome to TelCat, your telecommunications program. Copyright Craven International.

"Say Go or click on the word," advised the Cat. "Or say Quit to quit."

"Go!" said Spider.

"Firing up your modem," it replied.

The white rabbit appeared, holding its pocket watch. The watch hand swept once around the watch face, then the rabbit disappeared. "Modem okay," said the Cat. "Say 'Dial-in' for your dialing directory, or Quit to quit. For help, click on me, or type a question mark."

Spider shrugged and said, "Dial-in." A window opened on the screen. It contained a list of names, telephone numbers, and website addresses. All the library systems in town, including the university library. Bookstores and video outlets. Clothing shops at the fanciest mall. A couple of catalogue outlets she recognized. Right at the bottom were the words: *NetLink, Your Internet Service Provider.*

"What'll it be?" prompted the Cat. "Shop till you drop? Surf the Net?"

Spider hated shopping.

But kids at school were always going on about the Internet. Spider shrugged. "Net," she said.

"You got it," said the Cat.

Somewhere a telephone dialing system went *ping-pong-ping-pong-ping*, then the number began to ring. The white rabbit appeared, his watch ticking off the seconds. Suddenly, there was an odd vibrating sound, then a higher one, and the white rabbit disappeared. The computer emitted a high-pitched squeal that made Spider jump. Then it went doodley-doodley-doodley.

"Connection established. Hit any key," said the Cat.

Spider hit the space bar, and the doodling stopped. The Cat disappeared, and a new window opened in front of her. She read:

Konichiwa! / Ni Hao! / Hi! Welcome to NetLink.
Please login as "guest" at the > prompt until you have registered your own account.

Spider pecked out "guest" on the keyboard. A new window appeared with a registration form for name, address, and phone number. She filled them in. There was a brief pause, then more text scrolled up the screen. It said:

Hi, Sara Weber. You are already registered and prepaid for unlimited Internet access. Please choose a username (alias) for use on the Net. You can use your own name if you like.
Username >

Spider thought for only a minute, then keyed in "spider." What else?

A new line appeared:

Now choose a password. It can be up to eight characters long. You should mix letters and numbers.
Password >

Spider hesitated. It was all too much—she felt as if someone was stretching an elastic band between her eyebrows. So she typed in *"2Much!"* For a moment she thought something had gone wrong because no typing appeared.

Then, more text scrolled up. It said:

Registration completed. Remember, your password is a secret. It will not appear on the screen as you type it. Do not tell it to anyone, as this will enable them to use your account. Your e-mail address is spider@netlink.org. To browse the main menu, click on Menu, or on Quit to quit.

The main menu held a long list of choices.

Read mail. Read Usenet News. IRC. FTP. WWW. BBS.

Spider hadn't the faintest idea what any of it meant. "Get me out of here!" she muttered, and clicked on Quit.

Sayonara! / Zai Jian! / Bye! the screen responded. Then the words *No Carrier* appeared.

The Cat appeared, grinning. "Quitter!" it said.

"Get lost!" yelled Spider.

"I hear you," said the Cat and disappeared. The big screen became a mass of swirling colors again.

Spider looked at her watch. It was 12:30. She groaned. How would she ever get up in the morning? And she hadn't even thought about her English paper! Not bothering to undress, she crawled under the covers and pulled the pillow over her head.

> > >

He leaned back in his chair and stretched. Not bad progress for just a couple of days' work, he told himself. Wasn't it just too neat that Craven International happened to need senior code writers for some hotshot project? He'd seen the ad back East and e-mailed them his resumé. Talent, major creative talent, was scarce. Once they'd seen his resumé and had a look at what he could do, they'd practically begged him to work for them. The money was pretty good, too. He'd pretended he wasn't sure, of course. Said he'd had other offers. Let them sweat, trying to convince him. Or so they thought.

And now he was right where he wanted. Already he'd put out delicate feelers through the company intranet, teasing out passwords and sifting through locked files. It hadn't even taken him that long to break into Craven's personal data files. Wasn't that something? He'd dug out all the information he needed and more. The address, the NetLink account number, the works.

The school wasn't hard to find, either. He got that out of Joanna Craven's files. But that Par woman seemed to drive the girl everywhere. He'd deked out of work early a couple of afternoons, hoping to catch the kid alone after school. Just to make contact. But the big grey Mercedes was always right there waiting. Well, one point to Craven for taking no chances, he thought.

Then he'd tried phoning, but the Par woman always answered. He'd even written a regular letter, but in the end he hadn't mailed it. The Par woman might pick it up, or the girl might read it and take it to her. But there were other ways to connect, he told himself. He still had plenty of time.

Chapter 4

"You should see the crazy computer I've got," Spider said to Jerry Conway the next day. By accident they'd both ended up at the furthest end of one of the most remote cafeteria tables. Kids called it the Outback because no one who was anyone would dream of sitting there. Jerry had ended up there simply because he didn't notice where he sat, but the Outback was Spider's second home.

Usually, Spider didn't bother talking to people, but then, Jerry hardly counted as a person. Kids called him the Geek because he was nuts about computers. It was rumored that he had a microchip where his brain was supposed to be.

"Crazy how?" Jerry mumbled. He'd just taken a big mouthful of Garbage Delight, the cafeteria's pitiful attempt at stew. He was reading an article in a computer paper as he chewed and didn't bother to look up.

"How can you possibly eat that muck?" wondered Spider. It looked pretty awful. In fact, *he* looked pretty awful, with his frizzy red hair sticking out in all directions, elbows on the table, shoveling food into his mouth. Sort like an under-fed clown. Why on earth had she said anything to him?

Jerry swallowed, then thumped himself on the chest and shuddered. He glanced up at her before returning to his magazine. "Well, you didn't offer to share your caviar sandwiches, did you, princess?" he said.

"Don't you get on my case about Andrew Craven's millions. Billions. Whatever," Spider snapped. "Anyway, the sandwiches are just tuna."

He shrugged. "Gee, too bad," he said. "So, come on, what's so cool about this computer?"

Spider could tell from the way he said it that he wasn't expecting much. But even she knew that the Cat wasn't your usual kind of software. "It talks, for one thing," she said.

"Talks?" Suddenly, his bright blue eyes were riveted on her.

"You know, when you turn it on. It asks you what you want to do and stuff like that. Makes smart cracks, too."

Jerry whistled. "Voice prompts. I didn't know Craven was already into that with their PCs. I mean, way out R and D, yeah. But . . ." He looked at her suspiciously. "You mean it *really* talks? Not just a few standard words?"

"Yep," said Spider smugly. "It's positively chatty. I mean, this crazy Cat thing is. The white rabbit hasn't said anything yet. It just runs around with a watch and plays a trumpet."

"Whoah!" Jerry banged the side of his head with the heel of his hand, as if knocking water out of his ears. "Run that by me again?"

"You heard me. Cat. White rabbit."

Jerry looked impressed. "Well, you may not get caviar sandwiches, but you sure got something out of your filthy rich stepdad. None of that stuff is on the market. I'd know if it were. *PC World* is my main reading!"

"So, what *is* all that stuff?"

"Sounds like the voice prompts just substitute for mouse clicks or keystrokes. It probably only works for pretty simple commands. What does the Cat do?"

"Tells me how to do things and stuff. The white rabbit just makes announcements and times things."

Jerry snickered. "Animated icons! Sounds like your step-dad has quite a sense of humor. He's pulling your leg."

"I guess." Who'd have thought Supernerd had a sense of humor? The idea bothered Spider. Now she wished she hadn't asked Jerry about the computer. She got up and picked up her books.

"Boy, I wish someone would design dream software for me," Jerry said. "Uh, Spider?"

"Yeah?"

"If you ever need . . . I mean, if you'd like some help with the computer, I could come over sometime." He sounded embarrassed, but his eyes had a kind of beady gleam.

Invite someone to Fallingbrook? Not if she could help it! And where did he get off trying to make up to her just so he could try out her computer! She shouldn't have mentioned the Cat at all. "I'll manage," she said coolly.

"Yeah. Sure. Okay." Jerry picked up his magazine and swung his legs over the bench. "See ya," he muttered over his shoulder as he loped off.

Spider watched him go. She'd meant to give him the brush-off, hadn't she? So why did she suddenly feel kind of let down when he went?

Mia had an appointment downtown that afternoon, so she dropped Spider at the end of the drive. Spider crunched her way down the gravel road, swinging her backpack. It was cloudy, and the house wall loomed ahead of her through the trees, softly washed with light from wall sconces. Was it just her imagination, or did the lights along the drive get a bit brighter as she got nearer? She was sure they did. The Cat must have hidden cameras outdoors, too.

She palmed her way into the house and paused at the Cat's Ear beside the door. "Hey, Cat," she said softly. "It's me." A puff of warm air fanned her cheek, and somewhere a distant motor vibrated faintly.

Almost like a purr, Spider thought.

It was kind of nice to have the house to herself for once. Mia and her ESP were beginning to get on her nerves.

Despite her lecture about independence, Mia still nagged Spider about her eating habits, her clothes, and just about everything else.

"You're not my mother, you know," Spider had snapped at her the day before.

Mia had rolled her eyes to the ceiling, and exclaimed, "Well, Hal-le-*lu*-jah!" Then, when Spider scowled, she added, "No use pouting. Doesn't bother me a bit."

Then, unexpectedly, she laughed. "In fact my kid brother Carlito could give you lessons. His lower lip used to stick out like a dinner plate when I got on his case!"

"*You* have a kid brother?" Spider couldn't keep the surprise out of her voice.

"Sure," Mia said. "Thought I wasn't human, didn't you? I brought Carlito up after our parents died. That's how come you won't be getting away with much while your mother's away. I know how kids get up to stuff."

Spider had turned her back and stalked off. That's what you think, she said to herself. She actually hadn't had any plans to do anything, but now she'd put her mind to it!

Spider tramped down the hall toward the Treehouse. One of the doors, one that was usually closed, stood ajar. It had never occurred to Spider to be curious about the other rooms on the corridor before, but now she stopped and poked her head around the door. One glance told her the room must belong to a guy, for although the carpet was clear of litter and neatly vacuumed, the bed, desk, and chairs were piled high with guys' clothes and sports equipment.

Can't be Supernerd's, Spider told herself. No way he could be a jock. As far as she knew, he didn't do anything but make more millions. Anyway, he and her mother had a suite in the other wing of the house. So this had to be Carter's room.

A pungent smell lingered in the air. Aftershave lotion? Was Carter around somewhere? She hadn't seen his car, but . . . Spider sniffed again. Nope, more like bathroom cleanser spray. So the house cleaners must have been here and left the door open.

"Hello?" she called, just in case Carter really was around. There was no answer. Good. The last thing she needed was another encounter with that jerk!

She hesitated a moment more, then dumped her backpack in the hall and stepped inside. She felt a twinge of guilt at snooping in someone else's room, but remembering Carter's nasty name for her, she squelched it. All's fair in war, she told herself. And this was going to be war. Maybe. Probably.

The room, filled with sun, was just as big as the Treehouse, though only one wall was of glass. But it looked crowded because it held the most incredible heap of junk Spider had ever seen. There was enough sports gear to stock a store. Tennis rackets, a bag of golf clubs, and ski clothes. A pair of skis leaned against one wall. There were books, too, thick-looking textbooks, with folders full of papers tossed on top, spilling their contents all over the place. And clothes and shoes—stacks of them. It looked as if everything had been dumped and the door slammed shut on the mess. No one, not even she, could actually live in a room *this* messy, she thought.

And there was nothing, not one thing, to show that Carter spent any time here. Not a poster or a computer or even a shelf of CDs.

So what Mia had told her was true.

Just uses the place as his personal storage dump, Spider said to herself. Well, that was fine by her. The less she saw of Son of Supernerd, the better.

Idly, she flipped open a folder on the top of the heap. Inside was a transcript. She checked the date. Must be Carter's marks from last term. Spider scanned the line of Ds and Fs, grinning. Son of Supernerd or not, Carter clearly was no brain. Compared to this, even her report cards looked good!

She poked into more folders, but found nothing of interest. Her hand brushed against a sweater and, feeling its incredible softness, she picked it up and rubbed it against her cheek.

Wow! Must be pure cashmere, she thought. Carter sure treats himself to the good things in life. Like that rude-noise car of his. Bet the college girls all go crazy over him.

Then her eye was caught by a small, silver frame sticking out from under the mound of books. She tugged it out, sending the books cascading onto the floor. It was a framed photograph. Curious, Spider carried it over to the window for a closer look. It was a picture of a man and woman with a small blond boy about eight or nine years old.

Spider peered at it. The kid had to be Carter. Who else? So it must have been taken a long time ago. He was scowling at the camera.

Typical, thought Spider.

The woman was blonde and good-looking. The little boy looked a lot like her, so she must be DeeDee, Carter's mom. The way she was smiling into the camera was dazzling, almost as if she shared a secret with whoever was taking the photo.

And the guy? It had to be Supernerd. Holy cow, Spider thought. Did he ever look a lot younger back then. And not too happy about life, either.

The three faces stared back at her, each sending its own message. There was something fascinating about the photograph, as if it revealed a single moment in a story of which she'd never know the beginning or ending. Then she thought of the photographer clicking away at the wedding. What would his images tell about her private thoughts, her feelings?

Hastily, she turned to put the picture back. As she did so, it caught the light at an angle, and Spider saw that it had been very carefully ripped in two, so that the woman and child were on one piece, and the man was left alone on the other. Then the pieces had been taped back together.

Had Carter done it? Or had he just rescued the torn photograph and fixed it? Either way, it told her something about him. Something she didn't particularly want to know.

"Oh, rats," she said aloud, tossing the picture back on the bed. The last thing she needed was to feel sorry for somebody else. Didn't she have enough trouble of her own?

Suddenly eager to get out of there, she hurried to the door. But something made her pause and look back. For a moment she stared at the sun spilling in on the muddled heap of Carter's belongings; then she quickly closed the door behind her.

As she dumped her backpack in her room, she noticed that the Cat had sneakily put the Renoir back up on the wall.

Spider sighed. She'd deal with it later. She wasn't in the mood to go through all *that* again now. Somehow, though, she couldn't settle down to her homework. So she went down to the kitchen to look for a snack. She told the Cat to turn on the TV, then she settled down with a bag of chips and watched a couple of totally stupid sitcom reruns. Why be fussy? Anything beat doing her homework. Or sitting around thinking.

An hour later, she heard the whine of a car on the lower drive. Uh-oh!

She ordered the TV off, grabbed the chips, and hustled upstairs. The phone in her room rang as she entered. For a moment, she stood looking at it, then decided to ignore it. It couldn't possibly be anyone she wanted to talk to. Maybe Mia, calling to remind her to do her homework. It might even be her mother wanting to tell her how sloppily happy she was on her round-the-world honeymoon with Supernerd. No way she wanted to hear all that. She'd have to listen to it all when they got back anyway.

Five minutes later, Mia came rapping on her door. "Sara? Are you there?"

"Yeah." Spider hoped it didn't sound encouraging. She didn't bother to add, "Come in."

Mia opened the door anyway. "That was your mother on the phone."

"Boy, am I psychic, or am I psychic? I figured it was."

"So why didn't you answer? She was calling from Hong Kong."

"Oh, wow! Lucky old Joanna," muttered Spider.

Mia raised her eyebrows. "You'd better watch out for that thing on your shoulder."

"What thing?" Spider glanced hastily at both shoulders, ready to swat a bug.

"Looks like a great big chip to me," said Mia and shut the door.

Smart-ass, thought Spider. What business is it of hers anyway? Joanna was just going to have to get used to the idea that from now on she was Joanna. Not Mom. She'd made her choice and messed up Spider's life even more than it was messed up already. So Spider had a right to talk to her or not. That was fair, wasn't it?

If only her real dad was still alive. Then she'd have someone to go to. He'd have understood how she felt. She just knew it. Of course, if he were alive, she wouldn't have Supernerd as a stepfather, would she? So she wouldn't have all this grief.

Spider sighed and emptied her backpack onto the bed. She had to do something about that English paper. It was already a week and a half overdue, and the Bat was getting antsy about it.

She'd have to use the computer, for sure. The Bat wouldn't accept her handwriting anymore. Not after her last assignment, which he hadn't been able to read. She booted up the computer.

"Hi, Sara. What's up?" asked the Cat a moment later.

"You know what's up," growled Spider. "The Renoir is up!"

"You're sure you don't like it?"

"Yes!"

"Okay," the Cat said meekly. "I'll change the default settings." In an instant, the tomato soup can was back.

"That's better. Now, get me WordCat," ordered Spider.

The word-processing program sprang up on screen, and she found herself confronting a blank screen with a flashing cursor at the top of it. How was she going to manage to fill in even one page? And she was supposed to write a five-page short story. Something about feelings.

An hour later she still had only half a page, and it was stupid. She hated writing, especially writing about feelings. Yucky, woolly stuff like that made her sick. Even math was better. At least you did things that got predictable answers.

She deleted the text from the screen and sat there, glowering. Then she got an idea. The Bat wanted feelings, did he? She'd give him feelings!

Once upon a time [she wrote] *there was a girl who had a beautiful queen for a mother. Though her noble father, the king, had died when she was a baby, she and her mother were perfectly happy until this extremely ugly but filthy-rich prince came along. . . .*

Spider pondered. Well, not *perfectly* happy. She could sort of remember a time when she and her mother had fun together. When Spider was little, her mother had had to work days and study at night to get her degree. But she still found time for Spider. They used to do silly things, like have winter picnics in the park with lots of hot chocolate to thaw them out when they got too cold. They used to laugh a lot, too. But later, things had changed. Joanna had graduated from the Institute of Technology and gotten a job as a computer programmer. She was a whiz. Soon, very soon, there was a much better job, and after that she was putting in long hours and jetting off on business trips all over the country. There was plenty of money then, but never enough time for them to be together much.

And even when they were, nothing seemed to work out, Spider thought, gloomily. She was proud of her mother. Of course she was! But somehow she had turned into this shiny, glittering person that didn't belong to Spider anymore. Joanna had great looks, a fantastic job, money, an exciting life. Too bad she also had *her*—dumb, homely Spider.

She squirmed in her chair, remembering her mother's disappointed frown over Spider's latest report card.

"Can't you tell me what's wrong, Sara?" Joanna had asked. "You know you can tell me anything. We've always been best friends, haven't we? Remember how you used to call us Tweedledum and Tweedledee?"

Didn't she know how many years ago that was? Spider wondered. "Now is different," she mumbled.

"I don't see why. And I know something isn't right. I mean, look at you! The way you dress—grunge, or whatever it is you call it. You never wear the nice things I buy you, and you won't buy anything nice for yourself, either. And you're not even clean! You never used to be like that, Sara."

Spider had shrugged. "You say you want me to grow up. So why can't you give me some space? You just don't want me to do what I want to do."

"Be grubby, you mean? Mess up at school? You bet I don't! But it's not just that. You seem so . . . so alone. You never bring friends home or go over to their places. Don't you chum around with any girls at school?"

"What for?" Spider muttered. "All they want to do is talk about soap operas and guys!"

"Well, what's wrong with that? You act so glum all the time. Maybe it wouldn't hurt you to lighten up a little."

"Lighten up!" Spider had been indignant. "After the number you've done on me about getting good marks and making something of myself?" Gotcha! she thought, enjoying the baffled look on her mother's face. Let's see you get out of that one!

Joanna bit her lip. "Well, yes, of course that's important. But I never said you shouldn't have friends, have fun! And what's wrong with boys? You used to have lots of boy pals."

"Motherrr!" Spider rolled her eyes. "That was in grade three! We used to hunt tadpoles, for cripes' sake. Girls my age don't hang out with guys that way!"

Joanna smiled. "Well, hardly. But they do in other ways."

"What do you expect me to do? Go out and drag some guy over here by the hair?" said Spider angrily. "Why are you making such a big deal about all this?"

"I just feel something's not right with you. And it's not only me, either." Joanna waved the report card. "I've had calls from John Batsford and some of your other teachers. They're worried about you, too. Your attitude. They say you just don't try anymore. Your grades have been slipping ever since grade seven. But they all feel you have so much potential."

Spider shrugged. There it was—the killer P-word! Well, she'd soon set her mother straight about that. "You gotta accept it, Mom. I'm just not like you," she said. "Not pretty, and not smart."

"Sara, I don't want you to be like me!" Joanna said, an edge of exasperation creeping into her voice. "There's nothing wrong with your looks. Or your smarts. Anyway, have I ever said you had to get straight As? All I want you to do is your best." Changing her tone, she put her arm around Spider. "Won't you tell me what's really bothering you?" she coaxed. "It matters, you know. After all, you're all I've got!"

Oh, Lord. That line again! All it meant was that she, Spider, had even more to live up to! And she couldn't. She just couldn't.

So Spider shrugged off the embrace and said nothing. What was there to say? She couldn't explain the way she felt, even to herself. A kind of hopeless feeling as if nothing about her was right. She just knew she wasn't smart, so why knock herself out trying? And pretty? All she had to do was look in the mirror!

She could remember falling asleep on Christmas Eve when she was little, wishing she'd wake up the next morning with a face like her mother's, the kind of face that made people stop and look again. It had never worked, of course. Her own bony, peaky face with the spider mark always stared out of the mirror on Christmas morning. Now that she wasn't a dumb little kid anymore, she didn't even bother to wish.

It still hurt, though, when she met her mother's business friends for the first time. "So you're Sara," they always said. Then there was that quick glance from her to her mother and back. "She's not like you, Joanna," would be the next line. And her mother's lips would tighten.

You bet I'm not! Spider thought. Then gave herself a shake. She'd been sitting there staring at the cursor blinking on the screen in front of her. Talk about stunned!

And what did all that old junk matter anyway? Because after her mother got her dream job at Craven International it all got a zillion times worse. Andrew Craven, the weirdo from cyberspace, had zeroed in on Joanna. How could he help himself? He must have taken one look into those huge brown-velvet eyes and drowned! No problem finding stuff in common, either. They were both cyberfreaks.

No, what blew Spider away was that her mother wanted to marry Craven. Given his total nerdiness, it had to be the money, she thought. Her mother had gone for the big bucks. Go figure.

She stuck out her lower lip and blew a puff of air up under her bangs. Then she went back to her story. She managed to make it last for two whole pages.

. . . so the ugly prince shut the girl up in a huge stone castle and she lived there unhappily ever after.
    The End

Let's see what the Bat makes of that, she said to herself, clicking the mouse on the print icon. He was always wanting them to write slice-of-life stuff. Well, she had given him a slice. Truly.

At the main menu, the white rabbit appeared and blew its trumpet.

"Oh, goody," said Spider, as the Cat popped up.

"Eh?" it said. Then, when Spider didn't say anything else,

it added, "Craven International has downloaded some e-mail for you. To read it now, say 'Read.' To save it, say 'Save'."

Spider shrugged. "Oh, read, I guess," she said.

The mail window opened and the message appeared.

From: joanna@cravencomp.hk.com
Hi, Honey:

Sorry I missed you on the phone. We're leaving Hong Kong tomorrow for Singapore. Maybe I'll be able to reach you from there. How are you getting along with Mia? She's great, isn't she? I knew you'd like her.

Andrew says hello. I hope you like the computer. Why don't you send me some e-mail to joanna@cravencomp.singapore.com? I'd love to hear from you.

Love, Mom

"Yuck," said Spider.
"Come again?" asked the Cat.
"Quit!" said Spider.
"Ciao!" it replied and winked out.

Chapter 5

Spider banged the classroom door shut behind her. The Bat had kept her after class a few minutes to return her English paper. She leaned against the corridor wall for a moment, staring at the large red C– scrawled across the top of it.

"It's more than you deserve," the Bat had said to her. He pulled off his glasses and rubbed the bridge of his nose where they made two deep red marks. "Your writing's not too bad, but you're nearly two weeks late with it, and you've skimped on the page length. Not to mention ignoring what the assignment was supposed to be. It was supposed to be fiction. If I'd wanted your autobiography I'd have asked for it." He sighed and put his glasses back on. "Still, at least you handed in something. That's progress of a kind, I suppose."

Spider scowled and stuffed the paper into her looseleaf folder.

"Yo, Spider!" It was Jerry, the computer geek.

"Uh, hi." Spider made the words sound as uninviting as she could. She wasn't in the mood for company.

"So, how's life in cyberspace? Seen any more wildlife? Pink panthers, maybe?"

"Very funny," Spider growled.

"Hey, lighten up. I'm only kidding." He rumpled up his carroty hair and waggled his eyebrows at her.

Did he always have to look so embarrassed when he was around her? Spider wondered. If it were anyone else, she'd think it was because he was afraid he'd get a bad rep for hanging around with a loser like her. Except that Jerry was too far out of this world to even know about reps.

"Look, it's lunchtime."

Spider snorted. "Yeah, I know that." How dumb did he think she was?

Jerry's face got red. "I know you know. What I mean is, are you doing anything?" he asked. "One of the computers in the lab can access the City Free-Net. I could show you how it works."

"Uh, I guess," said Spider doubtfully. That's all she needed—more computers. But anything was better than eating her sandwiches alone in the Outback.

"Well, c'mon then," Jerry said.

The computer lab was empty except for Mr. Tan, the computer teacher. He gave Jerry a casual wave and went on with what he was doing at the other end of the room.

"He lets me hang out here as much as I want," said Jerry. "I help him with stuff sometimes."

You help *him?*

"Sure. We're always installing new software or something. He needs a hand sometimes."

"Must be *nice* to be a genius," she said, putting a bite into her tone.

"Uh-huh," he said absently, not even noticing the sting. He flopped onto a chair and booted up one of the computers.

I can't believe this guy, thought Spider. King-sized ego, or what?

Jerry began to type rapidly. A phone dialed, then rang, modems warbled, then an image with text sprang up on the screen. It read:

Welcome to City Free-Net.
Login Username>

Jerry rattled in a username and password, and a menu appeared. "Same stuff as yours?" he said over his shoulder.

"It looks different from NetLink."

"Different software, same stuff. You'll have mail, and newsgroups, and IRC . . ."

"Huh?"

Jerry shot her a pitying glance. "Thought you'd be into all that stuff by now. Well, you know mail?"

"Yeah." Spider pulled up a chair. "I've done that. At least, I got some e-mail. What's this other junk you're talking about?" She got out her sandwich and took a bite. Then, seeing he didn't have one, she offered him the other half of hers.

Jerry crammed most of it into his mouth to leave both hands free. "Show you," he said in a muffled voice, rattling away at the keyboard.

"How come you have to do all this typing? I don't."

Jerry swallowed the last of the sandwich. "'Cause this machine is a dinosaur. It's slow. And not enough RAM. It doesn't even have Windows, or a mouse. Leo—Mr. Tan—can't get any more money out of the budget for more up-to-date hardware and software this year."

"Mine's a lot easier."

"I bet!"

"Well, well, well. Look who's here. Creepy-Crawly and the Geek!"

Spider cringed. It was Greg Harris.

"Hey, Conway, aren't you afraid your pet computers will go all *buggy*, if you get me?"

"What do you want, flea-brain?" said Jerry. "Besides making yourself totally offensive, that is."

"Looking for you, maaan. My programming project has some problems and I . . ."

"Want me to fix what you've screwed up," finished Jerry. "Figures."

"Ah, come on," Greg wheedled. "My dad's really on my case about pulling my grades up. I gotta do well on this project, or he'll ground me. But something just isn't working. So, gimme a hand, will ya? If you can tear yourself away from your girlfriend for a minute, that is."

Spider jumped up, blushing.

"Cut the garbage. I'm just showing Spider some computer stuff," snapped Jerry. "Okay, boot up one of the other machines and put in your disk. I'll have a look." Then, "Hey, where are you going, Spider? Don't you want to see . . . ?"

"No, thanks, I've changed my mind," Spider said, and stalked off.

Behind her she heard Greg laughing. "What was it exactly that you were going to show her, maaan? Whatever you've got, she didn't seem to like it!"

Boys were such stupid, gross jerks, thought Spider. She didn't need any of them.

But that night, alone in her room, she couldn't help wishing she hadn't walked out on Jerry.

Boy, I must be getting soft, she told herself. I hate computers. Who wants to play those dumb games all the time? But Jerry was only trying to be nice. . . .

She decided to drop that line of thought pronto. It made her feel too uncomfortable. Anyway, Jerry was probably just feeling sorry for her. Who needed him? As for hurting his feelings, everybody knew he didn't have any. He was just a cyberfreak, a real mouse potato.

And the Net? Well, she wasn't brain-dead, was she? She could find out for herself. *If* she wanted to. But did she?

She thought about it for a moment, then shrugged and booted up the computer.

"TelCat," she told the Cat.

"Go for it!" it said and connected to NetLink.

Spider logged in and scanned the menu. Jerry had mentioned newsgroups. What kind of news? Current events? She hated current events. Oh, well. . . .

She clicked the mouse on *Read Usenet News.*

Reading . . . said the screen. Then an alphabetical list appeared:

alt.aardvarks.kinky
alt.anchovy.pizza.fan
alt.archie.bunker.die.die.die . . .

"Whaaa . . . ?" said Spider. Aardvarks? Kinky? She clicked on the line, just to see what would happen, and found herself dumped into a list of messages. She read a few, just to find out what was going down. Honestly, she thought, the things people will write about. What some of them had to say about aardvarks was truly gross! Spider chortled and mouse-clicked back to the main menu.

At the bottom of the screen were lines giving options. There was one for Subject. Did that mean you could select anything? But what? Then, suddenly she knew. She clicked on Subject and typed "star trek" at the prompt.

Reading newsgroup alt.startrek.fan read the screen. Then a list of message headings appeared. She clicked on a few and read them. These guys were going on about *Star Trek Voyageurs,* posting messages for and against. Some of them still hadn't got used to Commander Janeway.

"Get that broad off the bridge!" some guy had written.

The nerve! thought Spider, who adored Janeway.

Others were steamed about the multicultural crew of the *Enterprise.*

"Stop cramming political correctness down our throats," another one had written.

Still others were arguing about one comment or another, or trying to calm things down.

"Cool!" murmured Spider, reading greedily.

And the usernames were weird. Names like *demon, vamp, wildcard, beast. . . .* Well, her own was pretty weird, come to think of it, Spider told herself, grinning.

Then it hit her.

Nobody knew who anybody was. Some of these "guys" could be girls. Maybe even little kids! Nobody could see you. You could be anyone you wanted to be. You didn't have to be yourself. It was absolutely perfect!

She read to the end of the list, growing more and more excited. There were nearly a hundred messages, and boy, were they dumping on Janeway! What a bunch of fossils. Boy, would she like to tell them a thing or two! Then she thought, why *not* tell them?

There was a Post option box at the bottom of the screen. She clicked on it, and a message form appeared. She pecked in the name of the newsgroup and the subject "Janeway," then thought for a moment about the message. Then she keyed in:

Janeway lives! No matter what a lot of you coneheads think, Voyagers is a million times better than Captain Jerk on the old Star Trek. Maybe better than TNG. And if you weren't such a bunch of red-neck cretins you wouldn't worry about PC. Beam me up, there's no intelligent life here!
spider

She stared at the message for a moment, thrilled by her own daring. That was telling them! It was good, really good, and she'd done it by herself. She didn't need anybody to show her how. But should she actually send it?

Spider hesitated, then for some reason she thought of the Cat. "Go for it!" it had said.

Spider grinned and clicked on Send. "You got it, Cat!" she said.

The next night she couldn't wait to see if anyone had read her message. They had, all right.

Who's the freakin' newbie? one response read.

Other messages followed.

Crave this, spider—bug off.
I'm with spider. You guys are a bunch of coneheads. Give Janeway a break!

Who's this spider shootin' his big mouth off? Haven't heard from him before. Been lurking out there for long, sucker?

"Wow! I'm famous!" Spider chortled. She began to type.

spider to Trekkers,
Note that I don't address this to the dweeb trekkies who still drool over Captain Jerk's muscles and Spock's ears. I'm talking trekkers here, and even so, a lot of you sound one rock short of a load. And when I say rocks, I mean fossils. Let's hear it for Voyagers! Over and out.
spider

With a click of the mouse, she posted the message. There was no use hanging around waiting, she told herself. It would probably take a while to get some responses. Meanwhile, there were plenty of other groups to browse. She quit, went back to the main list of newsgroups, and scrolled down it:

alt.dingo.dog.fancy

Wonder if they're as kinky as the aardvark bunch? she thought, grinning.

alt.egg.salad.sandwich.fan
alt.flame . . .

Flame? A bunch of barbecue freaks, or what?

She clicked on the selection and scanned the menu of messages posted, selecting one at random.

"Whoa!" she said, reading it. Then she read another and another, and began to giggle. This was even better than the aardvarks. These guys were definitely far out. They were using words she'd never even seen written down. It was kind of like a war, with each writer trying to out-do the previous one in obscenity. It was gross, really gross. It was also pretty funny. You could tell these guys really thought they were something, using all those dirty words! Like a bunch of bad, little kids. Spider grinned, and began to type.

Crave this, barfheads [she wrote] *I've heard worse stuff in a grade school playground. If that's the best you wusses can do, you'd better change your name to alt.wimp. Get a life!*
spider

That oughta stir 'em up, she said to herself. This was fun! She hadn't felt so good in months. Maybe years! Suddenly hungry, she left the computer on, and padded down to the kitchen. All she could find was a couple of limp slices of ham and a can of Jolt Cola. It must be Carter's cola, she thought, munching on the ham. Somehow she couldn't imagine Mia knocking back that stuff. She punched the can open and carried it upstairs. She swallowed a few long gulps sitting in front of the computer. The caffeine hit her at once. Feeling tingly and wide awake now, she wrapped herself in her robe and hunkered down in front of the screen. There would be tons of other groups she could drop in on, and boy, were they going to know *spider* had stung them!

Chapter 6

"Hey, Spider baby. Caught any flies lately?" It was Greg and his bunch of goons. Ignoring them, Spider kept on digging in her locker, but she felt the familiar flush rising in her cheeks. Then her rummaging set off an avalanche of gym sneakers, books and other junk, and she scrambled after it.

"Aww, isn't that cute," drawled Greg. "Throwing all her junk at my feet. And looky here! Photographs. *Wedding* photographs. The cyber-king and Spider's mom, I bet!"

The goon chorus snickered.

Spider blushed even redder. She'd wanted to throw the photos on the floor when Mia had handed them to her that morning, but something in Mia's expression had stopped her. Determined not to look at them, she'd stuffed them into one of her books, planning to trash them later. Now it was too late. She made a grab for them, but Greg backed away, waving the photos tantalizingly. He glanced down at them and whistled.

"Well, scope this," he said, showing them around. "Who'd have figured that old Spider had a mom that looked like that? What a number! Wouldn't mind a night out with her myself. I could dig an older woman. Hey, must be tough on her having a bug-faced kid like you, huh, Spider?"

Rage hit Spider like a jolt of electricity. With a bound, she caught up with him and snatched the photos out of his hands. Then she jammed her face right up under his nose. "You creep!" she snarled. "Get off my case, you stinking scumbag!"

Greg's mouth dropped open.

"Ouch, ya got rocked, maaan," said one of his cronies, grinning.

"Yeah, man, the chick really burned ya!"

Spider banged her locker door shut and stomped off to the Bat's English class. She sat waiting for her stomach to drop back down from her chest.

Jeez, she thought, awed. Did I really say that? To him?

She had. The scowl on Greg's face when he entered the classroom proved it. And his pals were still grinning and riding him about it.

Greg shot her a poisonous look, then turned his back on her. His friends snickered.

Something poked her between the shoulder blades. "What's goin' down, Spider?" muttered Jerry from behind her. "Greg givin' you a rough time?"

"Not exactly," said Spider out of the corner of her mouth as the Bat called the class to order.

She scarcely paid attention as the Bat droned on about the poems of Alfred, Lord Tennyson. Is that all it takes to get them off my back? she wondered. Just talk the same cruddy language they do? She thought of the guys on alt.flame. She could give these jerks lessons!

Then she heard her name, and roused herself with a start.

"Excuse me, Sara," the Bat was saying. "I hate to interrupt your repose, but can you answer my question?"

"I wasn't listening."

The Bat raised his shaggy eyebrows. "I gathered that. So I'll repeat the question. May I have your comments on "The Lady of Shalott"? I trust you found time to read it last night as I requested?"

She had scanned it in the car on the way home, then forgotten about it once she got home and booted up the Cat.

"Uh, sort of."

"Sort of. I see. Well, can you tell us anything about the use of metaphor in the first part of the poem?"

Omigawd. Why wouldn't he let up on her?

There was a long pause, then, "Oh, I don't know," Spider said desperately. "I couldn't make head or tail of it. I can't stand that kind of garbage."

"Garbage?" The Bat sounded dazed.

"Yeah, well, you know," said Spider. "I mean, when Lancelot rides off, the stupid woman lies down and dies. That kind of stuff makes me hurl."

The room went deadly quiet. The Bat stood staring at her for a moment. Then he said, "Clearly you've failed to understand the poem. No doubt you need time to read it more thoroughly. Anyway, report to the vice-principal at three sharp."

"Just because I don't like the stupid poem?" challenged Spider. Something in her wanted to shut up, but something else wouldn't let her.

"Not at all," said the Bat. "Because you chose such a rude way of expressing your opinion. Your attitude is hostile, and it is disrupting the class." He turned away. "Now, Lauren. What do you think the image of the mirror represents?"

"Holy cats! What's eating you, Spider?" hissed Jerry.

She ignored him.

Everyone kept sneaking looks at her as if they couldn't believe what they'd heard. At first Spider sat there blushing, but after a while the corner of her mouth began to quirk upward in a lopsided grin. What a shock for the poor old Bat! For all the rest of the jerks, too.

Greg was waiting for her outside the class with some of his pals.

Spider's stomach tightened, but she stuck out her chin.

"Well, well. Having quite a day for yourself, aren't you Spider, baby?" said Greg, smirking.

"Shove it, toadface," said Spider, elbowing her way through the pack.

The goons fell about making coyote howls. "Shafted again, maaan! The chick's gone and got herself an attitoooode!"

"Better let her alone, Greg-maaan. The Spider has fangs!"

The vice-principal looked at her reproachfully when she showed up after school. "We don't usually see you around here, Sara," she said. She read the slip the Bat had sent along. "Offensive language? Disrupting the class? Something must be wrong. Do you want to talk about it?"

"No," said Spider, looking her in the eye. "I don't."

"Sara, are some of the kids bugging you because of your mother's remarriage?"

"I said I don't want to talk about it."

The vice-principal shrugged. "Suit yourself. But if you make a habit of this kind of thing, Sara, you're going to get into trouble. Big trouble. In fact, I think I just might have a talk with your mother anyway."

Spider grinned. "Aw, too bad," she said. "She's in Singapore."

That night Spider hit the NetLink's interactive games menu. Something called ImaginIt exploded on her screen in a shower of brilliant images. "Welcome to the universe of ImaginIt," a deep voice announced, and a man's face appeared. His eyes were dark and magnetic, and he had long hair and a beard.

"I am Zamor, the Master of All Games," he said. "Here you can be anyone you want to be, in any world of the past, present, or future! Please choose your username and persona *now.*"

She clicked on Persona. An option box with a list of choices appeared. They really meant it. She could be anyone! Spider typed in "Spider" at Username, then she began to shape her image. Hair—long, blue-black; Eyes—blue; Body Build—slender . . . Slowly an image began to shape in the portrait box beside the menu. A lithe, witchy woman with full, red lips.

"Wow, I'm gorgeous!" breathed Spider. Then she moved onto Describe Hobbies / Interests. "Star Trek" she typed at the prompt.

"Welcome, Spider," Zamor's voice said. "For a universe of adventure, why not visit ImaginIt's Spaceflux? Explore cyberspace. Carry out missions against the powers of darkness."

"Cool by me," Spider said, and clicked on Spaceflux.

Instantly, stars and galaxies bloomed before her on a field of deep black space.

"You have entered Spaceflux," said Zamor. "You will now proceed to the Command Hub to await your mission."

Spider found herself gazing into a room that looked as if it might belong on a space station. The room was empty, but the walls around her were covered with portraits and names of players in Spaceflux.

"Take time to look around, Spider," said Zamor's voice. "The green light means a player is in game. A red light means the player isn't online tonight. The amber means the player is present, but not yet in game."

It took Spider a minute to recognize her own portrait as she had created it. An amber light flashed beside it. Then suddenly, the light turned to green.

"You are challenged, Spider," said Zamor. "Do you accept this challenge?"

Spider clicked the Yes option.

"Your challenger tonight is Riff," announced the Games Master. "As you are a novice in the game, Riff allows you the choice of being power of light or power of darkness. Choose now."

Two outlines, one light and one dark, began to flash. Spider clicked on light.

"Very well," said Zamor. "From now on you may communicate either by command line or by clicking on instructions. Let the game begin!"

Instantly, Spider found herself zoon ing through space. A huge green planet loomed up ahead, then swallowed her up as she hurtled through its atmosphere.

"Whoaaa!" yelped Spider. On her huge computer screen, the illusion that she was about to crash was so strong that she shut her eyes tight. When she opened them she found herself gazing at a scene bathed in glowing green light. Her image and Zamor's were standing on the edge of a field. An emerald sun hung over woods in the distance. In the middle distance loomed a wall of darker green.

"Welcome to Viridian," said Zamor's voice. "It is the home planet of the Nazdak, one of the most intelligent races in the galaxy. Unfortunately, they are also one of the most warlike. They have conquered half the known worlds and stand poised to crush the rest. Only you, the agent of the United Planets, can prevent renewed galactic war."

Spider snickered. "Yeah, sure," she typed. "How am I supposed to do that?"

Zamor's voice was grave. "The Nazdak love only one thing more than war—gambling. They have challenged the United Planets to a game of Cybermaze. A representative of theirs will play Cybermaze against a representative of the United Planets. Winner take all."

"All?" Spider keyed in.

"If the Nazdak player wins, the Nazdak Empire will be left in full possession of its illegal conquests. If the Nazdak lose, they will withdraw to their pre-war boundaries. So the fate of the galaxy rests on your shoulders. Do you accept this mission?"

"Sure," typed Spider. "What do I do?"

"You and the Nazdak player will separately enter the Cybermaze. The first one to reach the center of the maze and claim the Greenstone is the winner. The winning player will then execute the losing player."

"Nice game," muttered Spider.

"Another thing you should know. Cybermaze is a game of skill and speed, but also of random chance. Part of that chance involves your weapon." He pulled a wand-shaped instrument out of the sleeve of his robe and handed it to her image.

"The way your power wand operates is random. It may be deadly or harmless. You can never be sure what will happen when you use it."

"Oh, swell!" said Spider.

"There's more. You will encounter various other random factors in the maze. Some may prove harmless or may even be helpful. Other can be deadly hazards."

Spider typed, "That's the craziest game I ever heard of!"

"The Nazdak *are* crazy," replied Zamor. "That's why they must be stopped. It's up to you now. Good luck!"

He vanished, leaving Spider's image standing before the towering wall of the maze. Spider clicked the mouse to move her image closer. Now she could see that what had looked solid from a distance was actually made up of millions of tiny green objects that shimmered and shifted before her eyes. The whole maze was alive!

There didn't seem to be an entrance. And where was the Nazdak player? He might be closing in on her already!

Spider sent her image charging straight into the wall of the Maze. It dissolved with an odd singing sound, then re-formed behind her.

Ahead, she could see two ways to move. One diagonal corridor seemed to lead directly toward the heart of the maze.

Too easy, she thought. Must be a phony. Instead, she sent her image racing down a shorter passage to the right. She stopped just before the corner and advanced one cautious mouse click at a time. The next corridor was empty except for a small plant that resembled a bush covered with white roses. So far, so good. She turned the corner.

As she got closer, though, the bush seemed to grow. By the time she reached it, it was as tall as the top of the maze wall on both sides and blocked her way. The white "flowers" began to look more and more like faces, and they all turned in Spider's direction. A tendril reached out across the ground and wrapped itself slyly around her image's ankle.

"Oh, no, you don't," she said, aiming the wand and clicking on Fire.

The wand turned into a bucket of paint.

"Oh, great," Spider groaned. "What am I supposed to do with that?" She clicked the mouse on the bucket, which flew into the air and dumped red paint over the "roses".

Tiny high voices screamed, and the roses turned red and then black. In seconds, the whole bush had crumbled into a small mound at her feet.

"Weird," said Spider, with a shudder. She moved her image quickly down the empty corridor. She had nearly reached the next turn when a hole suddenly opened in the wall to the right, and the Nazdak sprang out. It looked like nothing she had ever seen before, but she got a general impression of green, scaly skin, fangs, and claws.

"Whoaah!" she yelled, clicking on Back up, then on Fire again.

Her wand sent a beam straight at the Nazdak. It struck it dead on—and exploded harmlessly into a shower of roses.

The Nazdak grinned nastily and raised its wand, which turned into a laser sword. "Off with your head," it said, its grin revealing needle-sharp fangs.

Spider clicked on Duck and Roll just as a bolt of raw energy hit the maze wall beside her. Her image somersaulted through the hole it left, and Spider sent it charging straight on through the next wall beyond. Then she whirled, weapon at the ready. Nothing happened. The hedge remained solid.

"Whew!" Spider breathed. "That was close. This guy doesn't fool around!" Then she typed, "Stupid wand!"

"All part of the game," a voice said.

There was nothing in sight, so Spider clicked on View Rear. Instead of the Nazdak, she found herself confronting a giant emerald-green snake five times the size of a boa constrictor. It was coiled in the middle of the corridor, enjoying the last rays of the sun. Spider couldn't help noticing that there was an extremely large bulge in its middle.

"I suppose you're one of the hazards," she keyed in.

The snake yawned, stretching its mouth very wide indeed. Then it flicked its tongue at her.

"I am one of the random factors," it announced coolly. "Fortunately—for you—I have just eaten. *Un*fortunately for you, it was not the Nazdak."

It readjusted its coils, then went on, "Who *are* you, by the way?"

Spider typed, "Spider, of the United Planets. Which way should I go?"

"That depends. Which way do you want to go?"

"To the center, of course."

"All paths lead to the center—sometimes," it replied, uncoiling itself. "So it doesn't matter much which way you go, does it?" It slithered off into the wall of the maze, which dissolved around it.

Well, thanks for nothing, thought Spider.

She could see that the sun was definitely getting lower. Darkness in the maze was not a pleasant thought. She'd have to hurry. Should she go forward or back? The snake had just gone straight through. Maybe that's what she should do. With a click of the mouse she sent her image bounding through the wall.

She landed right beside the Nazdak. It hissed in surprise, then raised its wand.

"Holy moley, now I've done it!" Spider gasped, and fired first. A cloud of blue smoke billowed upward, screening the Nazdak from sight. She plunged through another wall and stood waiting, wand raised. Nothing happened.

"Way to go, wand!" she muttered.

Then she saw a door in the maze wall. The funny thing was that it was a perfectly ordinary door with a big brass key in the lock. Would it lead to the center?

Spider sent her image bounding across the corridor. When it reached the door, the key turned, and the door swung open, revealing a lovely garden beyond. Was it . . . ? Yes! There in the middle was a kind of plinth, and on it was a gleaming stone that reflected the sun's dying rays with greenish fire. It had to be the Greenstone! She'd won!

Eagerly, Spider moved her image forward, but suddenly it

was bathed in a sizzling halo of blue light. Then it crumpled to the ground.

From behind the door stepped the Nazdak. It looked straight out of the screen at her.

"Nice run, Spider," it said, grinning horribly. "But not quite good enough. So perish all enemies of the Nazdak. See you gaming!" It raised its wand in salute, then the scene contracted into a black vortex that drew her in and down.

A moment later, she found herself back at the Hub, her heart pounding wildly.

> > >

He was reading her e-mail. Handy, Craven's having put the name of her Internet service provider right in his files. Cracking her password had been no problem. Not for him.

Later on it would be amusing to let Craven know he'd orchestrated the whole thing from inside his own company. That would really rock him. Serve him right, too. Teach him that even his big bucks couldn't buy him everything he wanted. Especially things that weren't his.

He read some more messages. It was almost like sharing her mind. He had an inside view of what she was up to. What newsgroups she subscribed to. Where she went and what she did. He was getting to know her pretty well.

Spider, she called herself. The kid was really going wild, he could see that. Funny she hadn't looked the type, the glimpse he'd got of her outside the school. She'd looked a bit mousy, a quiet sort of kid. Now she was into all this crazy "spider" stuff, stinging people all over the Net. And playing wild games in a multi-user dungeon with a bunch of Rambos. Well, you never could tell, could you? The thought bothered him for some reason.

She was quite a character, though, he told himself, smiling. He'd found himself looking forward to seeing what she'd get up to next, and chuckling when she did something outrageous. He liked her spirit.

But that wasn't the point, was it? The point was to make contact with her in the time that was left, and convince her to meet him. After that, well, anything was possible, wasn't it?

Chapter 7

It was a couple of days before she bothered to check her e-mail. Craven International had downloaded another message from Joanna, this time from Bangkok. Spider deleted it unread. At NetLink she had mail from a *Star Trek* list she had subscribed to. And another message that was kind of odd.

From: smiley@rin.com
Hi, spider. You sure are enjoying your fun and games. You're going pretty wild out there. I'd really like to meet you. The two of us have a lot to talk about. No harm intended, honest. Mail me.
:=)

Weird, she thought, then she forgot about it.

Night after night she surfed into cyberspace. She checked out all the NetLink chat groups. Maybe, she told herself, just maybe, there'd be someone out there she could really talk to. But there never was. Mostly just a lot of people showing off or flirting. The Web was no better. Lots of glitzy sites, with plenty of music and videos and even freebies to download, but nothing human.

So most evenings she'd beam herself to ImaginIt. Riff was

usually at the Spaceflux Hub. It wasn't what you'd call a relationship, but it was better than nothing. One of these days she was going to beat him. Later, when she got bored with games, she'd drop in on the newsgroups again, just to keep things stirred up

And day after day her e-mail got wilder.

From: hoagy@esc.edu.ca
Hubba, hubba baby. Caught your image at the Spaceflux Hub. I can tell you're a gal who likes to turn up the heat. How about spending a little real time together?

From: boondoggle@cal.com
TAKE A HIKE, SCUMBAG! Why don't you take learn the ropes before you start throwing your weight around?

And on and on.

Spider read them all, grinning. She could say anything, do anything, and no one could do a thing about it. It was awesome.

One morning she was splashing her face, trying to wake herself up after a late night of surfing. She stopped for a moment, dripping, and gazed at her reflection in the bathroom mirror. She looked the same as always—her face half-hidden by lank hair, the small spider mark livid on her cheek.

Kind of like Cinderella the morning after the ball, she thought. If only I looked more like my image. Well, *tough*. Then a grin spread slowly across her face. Maybe she could do something about that. But she'd have to hurry.

She yanked off her baggy shirt and tucked a tight T-shirt into her jeans. Then she gathered her hair into a hank and twisted it into a side-slung ponytail. She studied the effect. Getting there, but . . . She looked around her room for inspiration, then grabbed a pair of lacquered chopsticks she had picked up in a dime store and skewered her ponytail knot with them. Definitely bizarre. That would give them all something new to stare at for a change.

But she needed makeup. She rooted in her desk for an old lipstick she sometimes wore at Christmas. Red. Good. She applied a scarlet slash of it and pouted her lips. Without all that hair around her face, she looked pretty radical. Sort of streamlined. She sucked in her cheeks to make her cheekbones stick out. Even better. Too bad she couldn't go around like that all the time.

She picked up her baseball cap and placed it on top of the computer. "Keep it warm for me, Cat," she said, heading out the door.

Mia's back was turned when she entered the kitchen. "Sara, what on earth were you doing up so late last night?" she began. "I saw your light on way after two in the morning. . . ." She turned around and stopped in mid-sentence. Cocking her head on one side, she took in the ponytail and the lipstick.

"Oh, nothing," lied Spider, stuffing her mouth with cereal. "I had a lot of homework, then couldn't get to sleep. So I read for a while. Didn't know it got as late as that."

"Yeah? Funny, you don't seem like the bookworm type to me. Well, at least I know you're in the house because I bring you back myself. Just make sure you're getting plenty of sleep, that's all. No late nights, at least on weekdays."

"Sure, sure, whatever you say." Spider shrugged into her backpack, eager for once to get to school. "Hey, we gotta go!" she urged, tapping her watch.

She could feel Mia eyeing her as she bounded ahead of her up the stairs. Nosy cow, she thought. Next thing she knew Mia's ESP might make her come upstairs to check on her at night. She'd have to make sure to close the drapes inside the Treehouse, and do without lights.

Once they were in the car, Spider thought of something. "What were *you* doing up after 2:00 A.M., anyway?" she inquired, just to let Mia know she wasn't the only one who could ask questions.

Mia glanced at her out of the corner of her eye. "Thinking," she said.

Spider waited for her to say more, but she didn't. Come to think of it, Mia was looking pretty crummy, at least for Mia. She was pale, and her eyes looked kind of funny, almost as if . . .

Nah, Spider told herself. Mia wasn't the crying type.

Mia's ESP must have clicked on because she picked up her sunglasses and slipped them on, hiding her eyes.

Spider passed Greg and the goons on her way to her locker. He wasn't saying much to her these days, but he mumbled something as she went by.

Spider stopped dead, and adjusted her backpack casually over one shoulder. She strutted back and planted herself in front of him. "Did you say something about me, little boy?" she asked sweetly. "I sure hope it was something nice, 'cause you know I'll flame ya if it wasn't."

Then she chucked him under the chin.

Greg blushed.

The goons fell apart, banging on locker doors and howling with laughter.

It's so *easy,* Spider told herself as she turned away. When I'm not afraid, he can't get to me. She felt a twinge of anger at herself. How could she have been so scared of Greg and his pals all this time? They were only a bunch of goons after all.

Lauren and some of her crowd had clustered down the hall, hoping for a scene.

And ditto for you, thought Spider. Sure enough, they made way for her as she sashayed toward them. She felt at least three meters tall. "Hi, kitties," she tossed over her shoulder as she passed. "How are the claws?"

In her homeroom, the Bat raised one shaggy eyebrow as she swaggered in. Jerry took a look and sank lower into his seat.

Spider smirked, feeling really good. I'm getting noticed, all right, she told herself. And they ain't seen nothin' yet!

That evening, she told the Cat to take her shopping. Usually, she hated it, but this way was a snap. No sales clerks trying to sell her stuff she didn't want or telling her things she liked didn't suit her. No Joanna, either, telling her, "Always buy quality."

No, now all she had to do was surf to the websites of the mall stores, click on the online catalogues, check out the photos on screen and choose. Then key in size, color, and her mother's credit card number, and it was done.

The results were delivered the next day, and the morning after that she tried them out.

A ton of makeup.

A micro-mini in scarlet leather and a matching scrunchy for her ponytail.

Black fishnet tights.

A tight black jersey.

A black leather jacket.

Eighteen-hole Docs.

Spider batted her heavily mascaraed eyelashes at her reflection. Shazam! It was her, but it wasn't. Or maybe it was a her she hadn't known she was yet. It wasn't exactly like her online image, but, hey, she was in the ball park. And there was no way someone who looked the way she did now would take anything from anybody. This should get her message across loud and clear. She began to feel a glow, just thinking about it.

Mia choked on her toast when Spider sauntered into the kitchen. "Don't tell me you're wearing *that* getup to school," she said weakly. "And what are those awful things on your feet?"

Spider grinned. "Doc Martens. Hey, you didn't care for the grunge look. Don't you like this either?"

"Just fine for hanging out on street corners, if you get what I mean," said Mia acidly. "I suppose it's no use my asking you to reconsider?"

"Nope," said Spider cheerfully. "A lot of folks are wondering what I'll do next. Gotta keep them entertained."

Mia clasped her hands and raised her eyes toward the ceiling. "Joanna, won't you please come home? Please, oh please!" she prayed.

Spider snickered as she climbed the stairs. She could hardly wait to give Lauren Pringle an eyeful.

It was worth the wait. Lauren looked her up and down, her face a study. "Well, I see you got some new clothes, Spider," she said. "At last!"

For once, though, the others didn't follow her lead.

"Rad boots," one of them said, eyeing Spider's feet.

"Yeah! Great skirt, too, Spider," another added. "Where'd you get it?"

"Le Château," said Spider, revolving slowly to show it off.

"Must have cost a bundle," a third muttered.

"True," said Spider, grinning. They'd given her a hard time about Andrew's money. Now let them chew on it!

At noon, two of the girls sidled over and asked her to eat lunch with them in the caf.

Say, hey! Spider told herself, pleased. She almost said no, just to be contrary and let them know she was no pussycat. But then she shrugged and accepted. Good-bye, Outback!

After a while, Lauren casually dropped by, just in case she might be missing something. Clearly they'd all been dying to quiz her about her new life, and they hung on her every word. Spider answered all their questions in a buttery voice. "Ooh yes, my stepfather's place is pretty special. Like, just unbelievable, really. Nooo, I don't miss my mom too much. . . ."

After a while the talk drifted to other subjects. At first, Spider only half-listened. Then Lauren and Chelsea got into a major argument about which of them was supposed to have videotaped the latest episode of *The X-Files* so the group could watch it together. It turned out that neither of them had, and everyone was really upset.

Lauren actually had tears in her eyes. "I mean, like, Scully's sick," she wailed, rummaging for a tissue. "She might have died or something, and we'd have missed it!"

Hello? Spider said to herself. She watched the show sometimes, but she couldn't imagine getting so worked up about it. These guys were so alien they might as well have been born on Viridian! Still, it did seem to matter a lot to them.

"Chill, Lauren," she said. "Scully didn't check out. I saw the last episode. They were on the trail of something totally new, see. . . ."

"*You* watch *X-Files?*" gasped Chelsea. "Tell us quick—what happened?"

Spider filled them in on the details until the bell rang. They hung on her every word.

It really was amazing, she thought, grinning, as she headed for her next class. All she had to do was talk tough and think of herself as slinky and cool. And act as if she cared about the stuff they did. Just walk the walk and talk the talk, and, baby, the world was yours.

Suddenly, everything was turning out just fine.

Except for the weird e-mail. Days passed, and every one brought another smiley message mixed in with the others.

From: smiley@rin.com
Quite the hot little flamer, aren't you? But watch out surfing, Spider. You never know what kind of sharks are in the water!

Seriously, I'm getting worried about you, kid. Nice girls don't get e-mail like the stuff you get. You don't have to be like that. Let's have a talk, huh? Mail me.
:=)

From: smiley@rin.com
Please give me a chance, Spider. Believe me, I only want to be your friend. Mail me soon.
:=)

After a while it began to bother her. Who was this guy? How did he know what she was doing? How did he know she was a kid? And why did he keep bugging her? Something about it felt creepy. Then late one night she got another message.

From: smiley@rin.com
I think we should get together in person, kid. Seriously. Just for a
chat. There's something important we need to talk about. Don't
worry, I'm harmless!
:=)

She sat staring at the glowing screen for a long time.

The next day she went looking for Jerry. She hadn't seen him outside of class for a while, but she soon tracked him down in the computer lab. He glanced up when she said, "Hi," then turned back to the screen.

"Yeah?" he said.

"You mad at me or something?" Spider asked.

He shook his head, but kept his eyes on the screen. "Me? Nah. Why would I be mad at you?"

Spider smiled her acid smile. "You used to at least say 'hi,' Jerry."

"Yeah, well, that was before."

"Before what?" She shifted her backpack and twirled the end of her ponytail with her finger.

Jerry gave her a disgusted look. "Before you went weird." He clicked the mouse, and the computer beeped a protest. "Blast, I lost it!"

"Aw, too bad," said Spider in a sugary voice.

"Listen," he said, turning to her. "If you want something, Spider, just tell me. If not, buzz off. I've gotta finish this."

"Jeez, you don't have to bite my head off," said Spider. "I want to talk to you."

"Oh, yeah? Sudden, isn't it? About what?"

"E-mail messages. Weird ones."

"Weird how?"

She told him.

Jerry didn't look too impressed. "Well, what do you expect? There are all kinds out there, you know."

"That's what Smiley says," said Spider. Maybe Jerry thought she was just being silly. There was nothing really bad about the messages, after all. Nothing obscene, not like

75

some of the messages she'd had in the newsgroups. It was just that they gave her a creepy feeling, as if someone was trying to come too close for comfort.

Jerry sighed. But he swiveled back to the computer and clicked on Save, then he cleared the screen and brought up the telecommunications program. "You'd better show me," he said. "Just type in the NetLink number and log in."

She did and brought up her e-mail listing.

Jerry started to read them, then stopped. "Uh, are you sure you want me to read your stuff?" he asked, turning to her. "I mean, it's private. . . ."

Spider shrugged. "I don't care. Let me bring up the first smiley message. It was about a week ago. I'm sure I've kept them all." She leaned over and scrolled down the list. "Here," she said, clicking on Read Message.

Jerry read and nodded. "So he always signs off with the emoticon?"

"The what?"

"The little gizmo. The smiley."

"You mean the punctuation? I couldn't figure out what that meant."

"Try looking at it sideways."

She did, and :=) became a little smiling face. "I get it. Smiley."

"Funny you haven't noticed emoticons. People on the Net use them all the time to show feelings. It's not always easy to know what people really mean on the Net because you can't see their faces. So people use these." He doodled on a piece of paper. "See? :=)) means very cheerful. :=(means you're angry, upset.

He scanned the list of other message titles, frowning. "Jeez, Spider, there's a lot of shouting going on. What have you been up to?"

"Oh, just fooling around. Got a few people pretty stirred up, I guess. What do you mean, shouting?"

"All those capital letters in the messages. That means a lot of people are plenty mad at you."

Just then the bell went.

"Nuts," he said. "Look, I'd like to look at the rest of those messages."

"You don't think I'm being dumb about this?"

He looked thoughtful. "Uh-uh. This guy's reading your e-mail. No way he could do that if he was just some jerk trying to date you up. Too bad your stepdad isn't around. He'd get to the bottom of it fast."

"Well, he isn't," snapped Spider.

Jerry jammed his hands in his pockets and leaned back in the chair. "So, you want to come back here after school, or what?"

Funny, she hadn't noticed before how very blue his eyes were. He wasn't really all that bad looking if you didn't count his weird hair.

Spider hesitated. She didn't like the idea of viewing her messages in the lab with all sorts of nosy people hanging around.

"Uh, why don't you come out to my place instead?" she asked. The words *my place* sounded seriously strange being said about Fallingbrook.

For a moment, Jerry looked startled. Then he raised his eyebrows and drawled, *"Moi?* A humble cyber-serf? To the palace of the emperor? Surely you jest?"

Spider rolled her eyes. "Listen, wise guy, are you going to help me or not?"

"Okay, okay. I'll come. It'll have to be later on, though. I have to finish a job for Leo first."

"Here's the address. It's the Riverside Drive bus. Go to the end of the line. You'll see the house number on the big stone pillar."

She snatched up her books and ran before he could change his mind. Or she did.

As soon as she got home, she checked her e-mail again. There was another smiley.

From: smiley@rin.com

Spider, I absolutely must talk to you. It's important to both of us. Make an excuse to ditch your chaperon. Meet me after school tomorrow at the Hut.

;=)

That was a café around the corner from Riverside High. He must know what school she went to!

And there was something different about the emoticon. A semicolon instead of a colon. What was that supposed to mean?

It was nearly five o'clock before she heard the door chime. She charged down the corridor and met Mia just coming up the stairs.

"It's someone I invited," Spider said stiffly. "A friend."

Mia scanned the viewing screen, then swung the door open, revealing Jerry. Spider could see her taking in the details. Unlaced hightops. Vest over a long shirt that hung over his ripped jeans. Goofy orange hair sticking out in all directions.

Jerry stood there with his hands jammed in his pockets. "Hi," he said, grinning. "I'm Jerry Conway. A.k.a the Geek."

To Spider's surprise, Mia just looked amused. "I'm Mia Par," she replied, waving him in. "How come 'the Geek,' Jerry?"

Jerry shrugged. "I fool around with computers a lot."

"Well, you've come to the right place. This house is stuffed with computers. In fact the whole house *is* a computer."

Jerry looked around, taking in a "painting" on the wall, and the touch screen by the door. "You said it," he agreed.

"Look," said Mia. "You kids want a snack?"

Spider cringed. Oh, lord! she thought. She's going to offer us milk and cookies!

Then Mia glanced at her watch. "It's getting pretty late, though," she went on. "Would you like to ask Jerry to stay for supper, Sara?"

"Well . . ." Spider wanted to melt with embarrassment. Jeez! Did Mia have to throw her at him?

"Would that be okay with your folks, Jerry?" Mia breezed on.

"Uh, sure. I guess. There's only my uncle. I'd have to phone him. That is, if you're sure. . . ." Jerry glanced sideways at Spider, as if expecting her to say no.

Spider decided to tough it out. She pinned a smile on her face and twirled the end of her ponytail.

Jerry scowled.

"Go ahead," said Mia. "There's a phone in Sara's room." She started down the stairs, then swung around. "Now don't get carried away, you two. I'm respecting your privacy, but no passion pit stuff, okay? And leave the bedroom door open."

"Yes, Ma'am," said Jerry, snapping a salute to her retreating back.

Spider groaned. Passion pit? What kind of oldie talk was that?

"She always like that?" Jerry asked.

"More or less," said Spider. "Look, if you don't want to stay it's okay. If you haven't got time. Or if you don't want to. I mean, I didn't know she was going to ask you. . . ."

Jerry grinned. "Chill out, Spider. It's okay by me. My uncle's cooking can be pretty gross. I don't often get a chance to give it a miss."

Spider shrugged. "C'mon then. The computer's in my room," she said, leading the way.

Jerry zeroed in on the computer setup without bothering to take in the rest of the Treehouse. "Oh, wow," he said in a hushed voice, staring at the huge screen with its random patterns of swirling colors. "Wowy-wow-wow! The holy of holies!"

He tore himself away from it long enough to make his phone call, then collapsed onto the chair in front of the computer as if he'd gone weak in the knees. "Man, " he said. "This is more than software. It's totally new hardware, too. Some kind of prototype, I bet. I've never seen anything like it. Would I ever like to take it apart and have a look!"

"Forget it!" warned Spider. "There's another smiley in my NetLink e-mail. Ask the Cat to take you there."

"Don't know if it will talk to me," said Jerry. "It may be keyed to your voice only. That's one of the big problems they're having with developing this kind of system. Different voices cause problems. Whatcha call the thing?"

"Nothing. Well, Cat, sometimes."

"Here goes. Yo, Cat," he said in a loud, clear voice. "You there?"

The Cat appeared, grinning its idiotic grin. "Hi, stranger," it said.

"Wow!" Jerry said, in an awed voice. "It can tell I'm not you! This isn't just voice prompts. It's more like artificial intelligence."

"It recognizes me anywhere in the house," said Spider.

"Incredible," Jerry muttered. Then, "Gimme NetLink," he ordered.

"Not so fast, " said the Cat. "Where's Sara? I don't take orders from just anybody, you know."

"Picky, picky, picky," said Jerry, grinning hugely.

Spider could see he was having a blast. "I'm here. Give me NetLink," she ordered.

"You've got it," said the Cat and disappeared.

When NetLink came up, Spider reached over Jerry's shoulder and logged in.

He scowled as he read the latest message. "The Hut's right near the school," he said. "Could be this joker's someone who knows you and wants to bug you."

"Greg?" wondered Spider. She'd been giving him a hard time, after all. Not that he didn't deserve it.

"Nah," scoffed Jerry. "Greg isn't up to tooling around the Net, much less reading your e-mail."

"The emoticon's different," said Spider.

"Yeah. It's a wink. Real sense of humor this guy has."

Jerry scrolled back through the messages, searching out the rest of the smileys.

"It's developed, hasn't it," he said. "Started out with just friendly advice. Now it's as if he really wants to meet you. And soon."

"He creeps me out," said Spider.

"Well, it could be anybody, you know. We're saying 'he,' but for all we know it's a 'she'."

Spider shuddered. "I can't imagine any female getting a kick out of bugging someone like this."

"Maybe. Well, the first thing you've got to do is change your username. And your password, too. Just in case."

"So he won't be able to send any more messages?"

"Uh-huh. And to protect your privacy and your account. Someone cracks your password and they can read all your mail, use your account, see where you've been—everything."

"So, how do I do it?"

"No sweat."

They got her password and username changed before Mia called them to supper. Jerry logged off NetLink and got up, stretching. Spider told the Cat to quit.

"Ciao," said the Cat, and did its slow disappearing act.

Jerry shook his head admiringly. "Way cool," he said.

Chapter 8

The next day there were no smileys. Spider breathed a sigh of relief. Whoever that jerk had been, he couldn't find her now. Spider disappeared from the Net, and a new persona called fireball went out surfing.

At lunch the day after, Jerry tore himself away from his computer magazines long enough to ask, "Still okay? Nothing new?"

"Nothing."

He nodded. Then he glanced longingly at the magazines and back at her as if he wasn't sure what to do next.

"Uh, you live with your uncle, or what?" Spider asked, looking for something to say.

"Yeah." For a moment, Spider thought he wouldn't say more. Then he shrugged. "I share his place, we eat together most of the time. I help him out at work, too. Other than that, he does his thing, I do mine."

"Sounds grim."

Jerry's face flushed. "Uh-uh. Cal's okay," he said. "He took me in when nobody else would." When Spider looked puzzled, he added, "After my parents skipped off, I mean."

Spider stared at him wide-eyed. He was trying to sound cool about it, but what he'd told her was really heavy. It had never occurred to her to wonder what Jerry's life was like. Or even if he had a life.

What would it be like to grow up without any real parents at all? She'd always had her mother, but she'd still felt she had missed out on something by not having a dad. All Jerry had was an uncle!

Jerry must have noticed her expression because he said quickly, "The Unk has actually taught me lots of stuff. He was one of the oldie Netters way back before it got all trendy. He runs the Dump down on Charlotte Street."

"He runs a *dump?*" Spider wrinkled her nose.

Jerry snorted. "Not a garbage dump, goofball. A place called The Hex Dump. Hex for hexadecimals. It's an Internet café—a place where people who don't have computers can hang out and surf. Worst computers and best coffee in town, Cal guarantees."

"Cool!" Spider twirled her ponytail. "Take me down there sometime?"

Jerry scowled. "No way. Not if you keep doing stuff like that. And shooting off your mouth all the time."

"Hey, don't you like the new me?" Spider smirked. "Everyone else does. Well, maybe not *like*. But at least I get a little respect these days."

"Yeah, because now you're as big a phony as the rest of them. I liked you better before. You were a mess, but at least you were real."

"Well, if you liked me before why didn't you say so?" challenged Spider.

"You weren't exactly friendly, were you? Now get out of my face. I don't want to talk about this garbage. I want to finish this." He buried his nose in his magazine.

Spider opened her mouth to flame him, then closed it. What did he know, anyway? He was almost as big a nerd as Andrew. Come to think of it, they had a lot in common. She swung her backpack over her shoulder and stalked off. But somehow she couldn't get as much swing as usual into her swagger.

"Your mother will be calling at five," said Mia, when she picked Spider up that afternoon.

"I'm busy."

"Uh-uh," said Mia. "This has gone on long enough. Why don't you stop trying to punish your mother? Anyone would think you were jealous."

"Me? Jealous of Supernerd? You've got to be kidding."

Mia shrugged. "I promised you'd be here. I didn't mention I might have to tie you to a chair."

"Very funny."

"Try me," said Mia, narrowing her eyes.

So Spider was down in the kitchen right under Mia's eye when the phone rang at five. "I'll take it in my room," she said stiffly, getting up. "That is, if you don't mind my having a bit of privacy."

"Fine by me. Just don't bother hanging up on her. I told her we were having trouble with the phone connection, so she should call right back if she got cut off."

Spider bit her tongue to keep from flaming her on the spot. It would be fun to zap her, but somehow she didn't quite dare to. So she stomped upstairs and picked up the receiver.

"Sara? Honey?" It seemed odd that her mother's voice didn't sound all that far away.

"Hi, Joanna," Spider said.

There was a moment's pause, and then her mother said, "How are you? I've been trying to get through to you every which way. Didn't you get my e-mail?"

"Nooo," lied Spider.

"That's funny. I've sent lots. And called, too. Well, never mind. Listen, I'm calling from Athens. We're flying from here to Rome, then to London. And from there it's over the pole and home. Wait till you see all the neat stuff I've bought for you. Something from every fabulous place I've been."

"Uh-huh."

"So what have you been doing?"

"All the usual exciting stuff. School."

"Tried out the computer yet?"

"Yeah. It's okay," Spider said—and thought, smugly, little do you know what I'm doing with it!

"I'm glad you like it. Andrew had his heart set on doing something really special for you. . . ."

"It's special, all right. Listen, Joanna, I've gotta go. There's something I have to do," said Spider. "Loads of homework," she added, thinking quickly.

There was a pause, then her mother spoke again. She sounded a little lost. "Oh. Sure, honey. I guess I'd better stop yakking. Just wanted to be sure everything is okay with you."

"Just swell," said Spider.

"Well, goodnight, then, Sara. Sleep tight. We'll see you soon. Andrew says hello."

"Yeah, sure," said Spider. "Well, g'bye." She hung up the phone, then slumped down in her chair. None of it was going to go away. It really wasn't. The honeymoon was just a kind of break before she had to get used to actually living with Supernerd. Just thinking about it was a downer.

Later, after supper, she did a little English homework— just enough to keep the Bat off her case. Then she got up, stretching, closed the drapes in the Treehouse and turned off the lights. That ought to put Mia on hold.

The Cat took her to NetLink, and she checked her e-mail. The usual junk. Fireball was having even more fun than spider had. Then, at the very bottom, was a message that froze her to the chair.

From: smiley@rin.com
Nice try with the password, Sara Weber. Won't do you a bit of good, though. As you can see, I know who you really are. Anyway, what's your problem? I just want to talk to you, Sara— that's on the level. It's really important. I'm serious. Just let me know a time and place.
:=)

He'd used her real name. And there was no way he could know that, no way in the world! She shrank down in her chair, staring at the computer screen. Up to now, she'd only thought of looking out at the world through it. Now it felt as if someone were staring back at her through its giant eye, watching her, trying to shrink her down to size.

The next day Spider pounced on Jerry in the computer lab. "You gotta help me. Even if you don't like me. Smiley's back!"

Jerry's eyes widened. "You didn't do anything dumb, did you? Like change your password and username back?"

"Do you think I'm crazy? And it's worse than before. He's using my real name now!"

"No kidding?" The expression on his face told her how bad that was. It made her feel even worse.

Spider shook her head.

Jerry frowned. "Okay. First thing, send a message to the sysop at NetLink."

"The who?"

"The sysop—system operator. Whoever keeps an eye on things. Now you've got proof that some hacker has got into their system. There's no other way he could have got hold of your real name."

"How do I do it?"

"E-mail to support@netLink. Someone's bound to take notice. Do it from here. Right now."

Spider plunked down in front of one of the computers and logged in. Getting connected to NetLink seemed to take forever. She found herself wishing the Cat was there to do it quickly. Then she was in. She began to type.

From: fireball@netLink.org
To: support@netLink

"Say you're reporting a breach of network security," said Jerry.

Spider keyed in:

Reporting breach of your network security. My password has been cracked twice, and my real name has been used in a message.

"Okay?" she asked.

"Tell them you'll be changing your username and password again," said Jerry.

Spider typed:

I'll be changing my username and password. My new username will be . . .

She puzzled over a new name for a moment, then typed *"hotshot"* and finished the message with the words: *"Please advise."*

She clicked on Send, and the message vanished into cyberspace. She sat back and shivered. The whole thing gave her the creeps.

"Okay, now go ahead and make the changes to your password and username. At least that'll derail Smiley for a bit."

Spider shifted to account setup and began making the changes.

After a moment Jerry added, "And maybe . . . maybe you should talk to my uncle Cal."

Spider noticed the hesitation. Jerry didn't seem any keener to have her at his place than she'd been to have him at Fallingbrook. What was *he* trying to hide?

"You mean at the Dump?"

"Yeah. Can you make it after school?"

"I guess so. As long as I let Mia know where I'm going."

"Well, give her a call, and meet me at the bus stop as soon as you can get there. It'll take us awhile to get downtown."

The Hex Dump Café was down in the oldest part of the city. Spider's eyes widened as she took in the garish signs along the street and the figures slouched in doorways or slumped on the sidewalk.

Mia would have a fit if she knew where I was, she

thought. And my mother would go up in a puff of smoke! It made her feel a little better as they picked their way along the sidewalk.

"Guess you think this is pretty grungy, huh?" Jerry shot her a sideways glance, studying the look on her face.

"It's okay," said Spider, hoping she sounded cool.

She realized she hadn't, because Jerry went on, "Don't worry, you're safe. It looks worse than it really is. There are a few tough types around, but a lot of these folks are homeless or just down on their luck for a while. That doesn't make them criminals, you know."

He nodded to a guy who was checking out a refuse bin in an alley. "Yo, Zack! How's the creative recycling?" he said.

The guy grinned and flipped them an offhand salute.

"Some of these guys come into the Dump to warm up when the weather's bad, so I know quite a few of them," he said.

Spider nodded.

"Here we are," said Jerry, pushing open a swinging glass door. "Home sweet home."

"You mean you live *here?*" Spider was shocked. The Hex Dump was one long room with a bar running down one side. It had an old patterned tin ceiling, and the bare wooden floor had a rakish tilt to it. A few people were perched on stools at the bar, sipping coffee, but most of the customers were clustered around a long bank of computers at the end of the room.

Jerry nodded. "Cozy, isn't it?" he said. Then, seeing her reaction, he added. "Well, I don't exactly live *here,* Spider. Cal has an apartment upstairs. Bathroom, kitchen, the whole ball of wax. Honest."

"Oh." Spider felt a little silly. Still, Jerry's life must be totally different from anything she could imagine. No wonder he was such a loner and kept himself to himself. She'd bet he didn't want anyone to know anything about his life. But he'd let her into it. And he'd said he liked her. Well, used to like her. . . .

"Let's see where Cal's got to. He's usually around playing

Net guru to the newbies. Hope he hasn't stepped out somewhere."

Left to herself, Spider looked around. The Dump seemed to be like a club where most people knew each other on sight. At least, she was attracting curious glances.

Spider tugged down her miniskirt and pretended not to notice.

Then Jerry came back. "Oh. Forgot to ask. Would you like a coffee or a pop? My treat—after all you fed me the other night."

"What's that?" Spider eyed a cup a guy at the counter was holding. It had a cloud of creamy-looking stuff on the top.

"Double café-latte-cino supremo."

"Whatever. I'll have one of those."

"Coming right up."

Spider followed him over to the bar. "You mean *you* make fancy stuff like that?" Being a barista definitely wasn't part of her image of him.

Jerry grimaced as he whipped off his jean jacket. "Yep. Gotta pull my weight around here, y'know."

The coffee machine was like nothing she had ever seen before. It looked like a brass rocket with an eagle on the top about to take off into space. Jerry pulled levers and steam hissed. Coffee shot out of one spigot and hot milk out of another. Somehow Jerry swooped the cup around so they both hit it at once. Then he put more milk into a jug and zapped it with steam. He scooped the fluffy cloud onto her coffee, topped it with chocolate sprinkles, and set it before her.

"Wow!" said Spider, impressed in spite of herself.

Jerry bowed. "A Conway masterpiece. Enjoy. I'll find the Unk."

She buried her nose in the milky cloud and sipped. Usually she wasn't crazy about coffee, but this was heaven!

The blurry mirror behind the bar let her keep an eye on what was going on in the room behind her. More people were drifting in now. Some wandered over to a row of video game machines, but most went down to the bank of computers. A lot of them looked like students. She'd bet there was no one here over twenty.

Where was Jerry, anyway?

Bored, Spider slid off the stool and strolled down to the computers. There were several free, so she sat down at one and stared at the screen, not sure what to do next. The whole setup was different from what she knew.

"Hey, could you tell me how to log into NetLink from here?" she asked the guy beside her. He was a weird-looking character wearing some crazy kind of hat. A long woolen muffler was wrapped around his neck and flowed down between his knees.

He glanced at her and sniffed loudly. "Gimme a break," he announced. "I smell a newbie. Sorry, kid, I'm busy. Go away and learn something before you take up space. Try again next week. Maybe next year."

"Sez you!" Spider retorted. "I can sit down if I like. There are plenty of stations free!"

A couple of people looked around and grinned, but one tough-looking girl, who sported a Day-Glo green Mohawk and a nose ring, scowled at Spider. "Try not to do anything too stupid, then," she said. "Gives the place a bad name."

Spider glared back at her. "Listen, motormouth," she said. "I've logged in plenty of times. It's just that my machine is different from these old dinosaurs."

"Listen to the chick dissin' the joint when she's hardly sat down," said the guy with the hat. "Now, is that nice?"

"Snarky, isn't she?" commented the girl with the Mohawk.

"No problem with the place," snapped Spider. "It's the company. So far."

At this, a sleepy-looking guy between the other two chimed in. "Oh, let her alone, Topper. You, too, Bunny," he said. "I remember when neither of you knew a RISC chip from a potato chip."

"Is that supposed to be some kind of stupid riddle?" demanded Spider.

"Sure," said Topper, grinning. "Isn't it, Bunny?" He turned back to Spider. "How *can* you tell a RISC chip from a potato chip, newbie?"

"I dunno," said Spider, trying to sound bored.

Topper raised his eyebrows. Then he snapped his fingers. "Dory? The answer is . . ."

The sleepy-looking guy, who had become absorbed in the screen in front of him again, looked up, startled. "Huh? I don't know."

"What do you mean you don't know?" Spider demanded. "What's the use of asking riddles without answers?"

"About as much use as having answers without riddles," said Topper loftily, turning back to his screen.

"I don't think . . ." began Spider.

"Then why go on the Internet?" Bunny snickered.

Spider jumped up. "This is the dumbest conversation I've ever had," she announced. "Bar none!"

Bunny laughed nastily. Dory, involved in his game, didn't seem to hear her. Topper merely lifted his weird hat, then turned his back on her.

Spider stomped back to the counter and flounced onto her stool. What a bunch of smart-ass jerks! Almost as bad as Greg and the goons, she thought. Just wait till I figure out the machines here. I bet I could show them a thing or two!

Chapter 9

A couple of minutes later, Jerry showed up with his uncle in tow. Spider's eyes widened. Cal certainly wasn't her idea of what anybody's uncle looked like. There was a lot of him—he was tall, and well over two hundred pounds, she'd guess. But somehow he didn't look fat. He was wearing black jeans, a fringed leather vest, and a short-sleeved black T-shirt that showed off a lot of colorful tattoos. His beard and mustache were streaked with grey, and he had a pony-tail almost as long as hers. He also wore an earring in one ear.

At least it wasn't in his lip or something, Spider reflected.

"Uh, hi," she said, tugging down her skirt and suddenly wishing she hadn't put on quite so much lipstick.

"Hi, there," rumbled Cal, holding out a huge paw.

Spider shook hands.

"Enjoyin' the scene?" he asked.

Spider frowned. "Not exactly. I tried to log on, but a bunch of creeps gave me a hard time."

Cal grinned. "Yah, they do that with newbies. Just give them back as good as they give you."

"Don't worry, she will," Jerry snickered. "Spider's pretty good at flaming people."

Spider blushed.

Cal's expression became serious. "Jerry tells me you've run into a joker in the deck."

"Yeah," said Spider, wondering if he'd think she was making a fuss about nothing. "It's probably no big deal, but . . ."

Cal hoisted himself onto a stool, which creaked in protest. "Jerry must think there's something to it, or he wouldn't have brought you here. 'Cause he doesn't bring *anybody* here." He glanced at Jerry, who dropped his eyes to the floor and shuffled his feet. "So, tell me," Cal went on. "From the beginning."

"Well, my stepfather gave me this computer. . . ." When she got to the part about goofing off on the Net, she hesitated for a moment, then plunged on.

Cal groaned and rolled his eyes toward the ceiling. "Talk about stirring up hornets with a stick! It's a wonder only one crazy has zeroed in on you!"

"But I thought . . . I thought nobody knew who you were. You could be anyone you wanted to be. . . ." Spider's voice trailed off.

"So you decided to play electronic poltergeist." Cal gave her a level look. "That was pretty stupid! There are plenty of hackers out there who have the smarts to find out who you are if they really decide to come after you."

"I guess I didn't think," mumbled Spider.

"I guess." Cal thought for a moment. "Well, Jerry was right to have you tip off the folks at NetLink. Smiley might be inside the company, and who knows what he may do? If he can crack one password, he can crack others."

"Is there anything else we can do?" asked Jerry. "I mean besides checking out what NetLink has to say? We already changed her password and username again."

Cal thought for a moment. "Don't think there's any use talking to the police—not yet. The guy hasn't done anything to her. It's kind of like obscene phone calls—they just tell you to get an unlisted number. Of course, if NetLink catches up with this guy they may be able to nail him with some charge."

"Is there anything else we can do?" asked Spider. It felt awfully good to say "we."

"What about a bozo filter?" suggested Jerry.

Cal nodded. "It's worth a try. NetLink will install one on her account if she asks them to. But maybe she needs one on her home computer, too, in case Smiley tries to send her e-mail some other way." He turned to Spider. "You ever get mail that doesn't come via NetLink?"

Spider blinked. "Yeah, I guess I do. I've had messages from Andrew and my mother. They seem to come directly from Craven International."

"So you've got an e-mail address there, too. It's a bozo filter for you, then. After all, if Smiley can hack into NetLink, he might be able to hack into Craven." Cal scratched his bearded chin and pondered. Then he added, "Maybe we should go a little farther than that, too, and Finger him. The biter bit."

"Yeah! Why didn't I think of that?" said Jerry.

"Excuuuse me," said Spider. "What's all this stuff about bozos and fingers?"

"Okay," said Cal. "Bozo filter. That's as in Bozo the Clown. If some clown's bugging you, you can install software to screen out messages from that person only."

"And Finger is a UNIX command," Jerry cut in. "UNIX is the operating system that runs the big Internet server computers."

"Duh," said Spider.

Jerry grinned. "Okay, okay. Well, Finger is just a way of finding out certain kinds of information about people on the Net."

"Maybe I should just e-mail the guy and tell him to get lost," said Spider, nibbling a fingernail.

"Don't," said Cal. "That's what he wants. To get you involved with him."

"If we can find out something about him first and then

let him know we know who he really is, maybe that will discourage him," said Jerry.

"Okay," said Spider. "Let's put the finger on him!"

Cal slid off his stool and led the way down to the computers. All the stations were full.

"Sorry, Topper," he said, placing a hamlike hand on the shoulder of the guy in the hat. "Have to bump you for a while."

"Aw, maaan, I hardly just sat down," protested the boy.

"Them's the breaks," said Cal, lifting the chair from under him. "It'll be all yours just as soon as we're finished. Go have a coffee on the house."

Topper shot Spider a dirty look and slouched off. Cal sat down in front of the computer. His fingers danced over the keys, clearing the screen of Topper's search and inputting new commands.

Suddenly, the screen was clear except for a $ prompt.

"He's got the UNIX shell now," explained Jerry. "That lets him do Finger and a whole lot of other stuff."

Cal typed: *finger smiley@rin.com.* Spider and Jerry leaned over his shoulders, waiting.

Finger search, responded the screen. Then, *Mistyped username.*

"But you didn't mistype," said Spider.

"Yah," said Cal. "I'll try again anyway."

Mistyped username, repeated the screen.

Cal swore softly under his breath. "He's smart—I have to give him that," he muttered.

Spider glanced at Jerry.

"It means *smiley* isn't a regular username anywhere on the Internet," he explained.

"Huh? But . . . ?"

"Yeah, I know. This is really weird." Jerry sounded puzzled.

"I'm trying his company name now," said Cal.

He typed: *nic@rin.com.*

The computer responded: *unknown company*

"Great balls of fire!" roared Cal. "That's a dud, too."

"He knows you might try to send somebody after him." Jerry was thinking aloud. "So he uses a phony address. He must have set it up so that if you mail him it gets bounced to his real address. How the heck does he do it?"

Cal sat scowling at the screen, his eyebrows knitted. "I dunno. He might have found a bug in the software that runs the server computers and figured out how to use it." He heaved a sigh. "Anyway, I bet NetLink's run into the same problem we have," he said. "Let's see." He connected to NetLink, and motioned Spider to replace him in front of the screen. "Login and go to your e-mail," he told her.

Spider obeyed. Sure enough, she had new mail.

From: support@netlink.org
Unable to trace sender smiley@rin.com. Note you have changed username and, we assume, your password. We are checking to see if other accounts have been tampered with. Will keep you posted.

"Well, thanks for nothing," sighed Spider.

"We haven't done much better," Cal reminded her. He stood stroking his beard and frowning.

"You don't think we've seen the last of the guy, Unk?" asked Jerry.

Cal slowly shook his massive head. "No. Finger didn't give us what we wanted, but it did tell us two things. First, the guy's a major hacker, or he wouldn't be able to do what he has done. Setting up a phony e-mail address ain't easy. Second, he's gone to the trouble of cooking this up just for Spider. *Why?* It doesn't make sense for just the average Net grudge. There's gotta be another reason."

A lump of worry settled in Spider's stomach. "What do I do now?" she asked.

"First, get the bozo filters installed," said Cal. "When you get home, e-mail support at NetLink and ask them to filter out all further messages from Smiley. "

Jerry went over to a rack of software, and returned with a

disk shrink-wrapped in plastic. "Here's the 'ware for your own computer," he said, holding it out. "It's pretty easy to install—just stick it in your floppy drive and follow the on-screen directions."

Spider took the disk and turned to Cal. "Gee, thanks. How much do I owe you for this?" she asked.

Cal shrugged. "Nothin'. It's shareware. If it works for you and you go on using it, you're supposed to mail some money to the company that wrote it."

"Kind of an honor system," Jerry put in.

"Cool," said Spider. Imagine people trusting each other for something like that!

"Let me know at school tomorrow if you have any trouble installing the filter," said Jerry.

"And now," said Cal, "we'd better think about getting you home. How's about if I give you a ride?"

"Great! I'll call Mia and tell her I'm on my way," said Spider. No way did she want Mia picking her up here. Once she got an eyeful of the Dump, Spider would never hear the end of it.

Spider made her call and went outside with Jerry to wait for Cal. In a few minutes, he appeared out of the alley, wearing a leather jacket, helmet and boots. He was wheeling a huge black and chrome motorcycle.

"Oh, lord," moaned Spider.

"Cool, huh?" said Jerry. "It's an old Harley he's fixed up. It's cost him thousands. Cal won't let me lay a finger on it."

"Uh . . . I've never been on a motorcycle," quavered Spider.

"It's a blast. You'll love it!" said Jerry. "Well, so long. See you tomorrow."

Spider nodded glumly and walked over to where Cal sat astride the Harley.

"Helmet on," he said, holding one out with a grin. She had the uncomfortable feeling he knew exactly how she felt about his motorcycle. "Now just sling your leg over and sit here behind me," he added. "Your feet go there. Hang on to me tight."

Spider obeyed, stretching her arms tight around Cal's leather-clad sides. It felt exactly like hugging a steel barrel. Whatever this guy was, it wasn't flabby.

The people in the street were bantering with Cal. Jerry waved from the doorway of the Dump. Spider didn't even try to wave back. She hung on as hard as she could, and pressed her helmeted head against Cal's back.

Then they were off, with a roar and a rush unlike anything she had ever experienced before. Cal wove his way expertly through the traffic, leaning first one way, then another.

At first Spider kept her eyes closed out of sheer terror. Then she opened them a slit. They were leaving the downtown area now and merging onto the freeway. Faster and faster, until they seemed to be flying. Spider couldn't even hear the noise anymore, just the rush of the wind. It felt so free.

"Whoaaa!" she yelped, as Cal swung the cycle onto an exit ramp. But her voice was whipped away by the wind.

They were slowing, now, as Cal made the turn onto Riverside Drive. Spider thumped him on the arm and pointed ahead to the stone pillars at the end of the road. Cal's helmeted head nodded.

The cycle slowed and turned easily onto the gravel drive. Minutes later, Cal pulled up in front of the house, bringing the cycle to a gentle stop.

Mia was standing in the doorway. She looked flabbergasted.

Spider, recovering, suddenly felt quite pleased with herself.

"I thought I heard . . . something," Mia began.

Spider lurched off the cycle and unbuckled her helmet. Her legs felt rubbery, but she willed them to hold her up.

"Cal, this is Mia Par," she said. "She's staying with me while my mother is away."

"Hello, Miz Par," said Cal, pulling off his leather gauntlet and offering his paw. "Didn't want Spider taking the bus from downtown this late on."

Mia shook Cal's hand. "That was kind of you, Mr. . . . ?" Her tone of voice made it clear that she wanted an answer.

"Just call me Cal." He winked at Spider and waved his gauntlet. "So long, kid. Keep in touch. Be seein' you." He kicked the Harley into life and roared off.

"Who on earth was *that?*" asked Mia, staring after him. "I thought you said Jerry's uncle was going to drive you."

"He did. That's him," said Spider, grinning.

> > >

He tented his fingers and sat back staring at the glowing screen. Smart kid. She was trying just about everything to shake him off. One thought was beginning to trouble him, though. Unless she knew more than he thought she did, she must be getting help from someone. That could be bad, he reflected. Suppose she went to the cops? He didn't want the law breathing down his neck. That would ruin everything.

Anyway, it was a good thing he'd sent all the messages via NetLink. There was no data track here at Craven, and he couldn't be traced unless someone caught him in mid-message. Which was almost impossible.

But he wasn't getting anywhere. The kid wasn't listening to him. He'd thought he could gain her confidence without scaring her off and then set up a meeting. But she hadn't sent him even one message, hadn't showed up at the Hut though he'd waited around on several different days. Why did she have to be so hard to convince? The one thing he couldn't tell her was the truth. Not yet. If he did, she'd be sure to tell someone, and he couldn't risk that.

He shifted uneasily in his chair. He was running out of time, too. The Cravens wouldn't stay away forever, and once they were back it would be game over. He'd never get near her, never get another chance.

Well, if she wouldn't come to him, he'd have to find a way to get to her. And it would have to be soon.

Chapter 10

A day passed, then another. No new smileys. Spider felt as if some tightly coiled spring inside her was beginning to unwind.

"Maybe the bozo filter's done it," said Jerry when she stopped him in the hall to tell him. "You told NetLink, too?"

"Yeah. They said they could run something from their end to screen him out."

Then it happened again. Spider checked her e-mail, and there was a new message.

From: smiley@rin.com
C'mon, Sara, stop fooling around! You know I'll find you, what-ever name you try to hide under. Who needs all this? Why not just agree to meet me somewhere? I only want to talk to you. After that, I won't bug you anymore. That's a promise!
:=)

Should she do what he asked just to get him off her case? For a moment Spider considered it. She could meet him at the Hut or somewhere else that was public. He couldn't do her any harm that way, could he?

100

She shivered. The creepy feeling was too strong. She didn't want to do it.

"Jerry, he's back!" Spider hissed over her shoulder in English class the next day.

"You're kidding!" said Jerry.

"Wish I were! "

"Cripes!"

Then the sound of a throat being cleared loudly made them both jump.

"Ah, thank you," said the Bat. "Good of you to give me your attention. Now as to my question about *Romeo and Juliet*. Jeremy, would you care to explain your odd answer?"

"It was nothing, sir. I just said, 'Cripes!'"

"Cripes. I see. Not the answer I was looking for. Not really an explanation of Romeo's point of view."

A titter ran around the class.

"Was I being funny, class?" the Bat asked, glowering around. "I hope not."

Lauren Pringle squeaked, "Uh, no, sir. It's not you. It's just that Spider and Jerry have been Romeo and Juliet lately. Sort of. I mean, hanging out together a lot . . ." Her voice trailed away and she giggled.

Spider blushed, and Jerry sank down lower behind his desk.

The Bat raised his beetling eyebrows. "So you think that gives them a special expertise, as it were." He swung back to Jerry. "Well, expert or not, I'd like to hear your thoughts on Romeo, Jeremy."

"I dunno," mumbled Jerry. "Sorry, sir. I guess I didn't hear your question."

The Bat sighed. "Sara?"

"Me either, sir."

"I see. Well, I'm sure what you have to say to each other is far more interesting than anything you expect to hear from me. Still, try to postpone your private conversations until after class. Clear?"

"Yessir," said Jerry.

"Yessir," echoed Spider. "You old creep," she added under her breath as he turned away.

Jerry kicked her feet from behind. "Knock it off, Spider," he hissed. Then he smiled innocently at the Bat, who had swung around again.

It didn't do any good.

"That'll cost you an extra page of written analysis of Act II, Scene II of the play," he snapped. "You, too, Sara. In fact, make that two pages each. In addition to the class assignment, that is."

They groaned.

Jerry caught up with her again in the cafeteria. "Listen, Spider," he said. "I called Cal. I told him how upset you are, and he invited you for dinner."

"Tonight?"

"Sure. Why not? The way he cooks doesn't take much preparation."

"I'll have to ask. I'll phone you later."

When Mia and Spider got home, Carter's Porsche was in the driveway. They found him down in the kitchen, feet up on the table, guzzling a can of Jolt. When he caught sight of Spider, his eyes widened and he looked her up and down. "Whoaaa, Bugface," he drawled, "hasn't Halloween come a bit early? Or are you planning a whole new career in horror movies?"

Stung, Spider shot back, "Aw, stuff it, Rock Ears." She nudged the tin of Jolt with the tip of her finger. "What're you trying to do, jump-start your brain?"

Carter blinked, but before he could reply, Mia cut in, "I've warned you about calling Sara by that ugly name, Carter!" She frowned at him. "And what are you doing here, anyway? You said you wouldn't be around while Andrew was away."

Carter shrugged. "Hey, can I help it if I crave your company sometimes, Ice Queen? And the brat's?" He jerked his thumb at Spider, who rolled her eyes.

"Oh, sure," snapped Mia. "Kicked out of your dorm again

is more like it, yes? Broke one rule too many and got caught. Well, that's just great. Now I'll have the two of you on my hands. Maybe I should just grab some guy and take off on a long honeymoon myself."

"You missed your chance. Dad's already on his," smirked Carter.

"Zip that lip, buster," snapped Mia.

Wow! thought Spider. He really does try to get her goat! Then, seeing a chance to change the subject, she said briskly, "Well, you won't need to feed me tonight, anyway, Mia, 'cause Jerry's uncle has invited me for dinner."

Mia raised her eyebrows. "At that . . . whatever it's called?"

"The Hex Dump," Spider reminded her. "Not exactly. At their apartment upstairs."

Carter whistled. "You hanging out at the Dump these days, kid? Lotta the computer nerds at college go there."

Mia rounded on Spider. "Exactly what kind of place is this . . . Dump? I thought you told me it's a coffee house."

"Well, it is. Plus a few computers," Spider hedged.

"Not to mention a video arcade," said Carter, grinning.

"It's not an arcade! There are a few video game machines, is all," snapped Spider. "People just play them while they're waiting for a turn at the computers."

Mia looked troubled. "I'm not sure that sounds like the kind of place you should be going, Sara. Your mother . . ."

"Give me a break! You've met Jerry. He's okay, isn't he?"

"Jerry's fine," said Mia.

"And you've met Cal."

"I certainly have," said Mia coolly.

"It's not fair!" accused Spider. "You're just being snooty because Cal is . . . different."

"It's not really a question of my likes and dislikes, Sara. I'm responsible to Andrew and your mother for looking after you. I think she'd worry if she knew you were riding around town on the back of a motorcycle."

"Motorcycle?" whooped Carter. "Bug . . . I mean, Sara?"

Mia ignored him. "I'm sorry to disappoint you. It was kind of . . . Cal . . . to invite you. But the answer is no."

"But I *have* to go!" Spider pleaded. "It's really important. If you knew . . ."

"If I knew *what?*" Mia's eyes narrowed.

Spider could tell her ESP had switched on. Antennas practically sprouted from her ears. "Oh . . . nothing," she babbled. "I just mean, I really, really want to go."

To Spider's surprise, Carter spoke up. "Aw, give the kid a break, Mia. I was only kidding about the Dump. There's nothing wrong with it. From what I hear the guy runs a squeaky-clean operation. No drugs or alcohol allowed in the place. Not even beer. Just coffee and computers. What a snore! No wonder I don't go there."

"That *is* some recommendation," said Mia.

"Pleeease," begged Spider.

Mia hesitated. "Well, maybe it would be all right. On one condition. Carter drops you off and picks you up later."

Carter threw his hands up in mock horror. "Hey, no way. Why should I baby-sit the brat?" he protested.

"Because you're such a sweetie, and you just love making yourself useful, don't you?" Mia pinched his cheek.

Carter looked disgusted. Then he shrugged. "Okay, okay. You're on, brat. But you owe me one."

Spider grinned and twirled her ponytail. "Anytime, Cementhead," she said.

"Jeez," Carter said, turning to Mia. "The kid's got a mouth on her."

"That makes two of you," Mia shot back.

He was still complaining when he drove Spider downtown.

"Oh, knock it off, Carter," Spider said impatiently. "There's something I want to know."

"Yeah? What's that?" Carter shot her a curious look.

"About your father and Mia. That crack you made. And you said something like it before, I remember. What's the story?"

"No story. Oh, she's crazy about him, of course. Always has been, as long as I can remember. Everyone knows it but Dad. He may be a computer genius, but he's too dumb about people to notice stuff like that."

Carter's voice had an edge to it. Spider sneaked a look at him out of the corner of her eye, remembering the angry little boy staring out of the old photograph. Maybe being Son of Supernerd wasn't all that much fun, despite his fancy lifestyle. Maybe he didn't like having to live up to someone all the time any more than she did. Then another thought struck her. Maybe he thought nobody even cared about him anymore. Not with his mother remarried, and a new stepmother and her kid taking over his father's life.

After a moment, Carter went on, "No, to Dad, Mia's just the girl next door—his oldest and best friend. Absolutely nooo chemistry as far as he's concerned. In fact, no one thought Dad would ever remarry." He frowned. "He's always said he'd had enough, after he and Mom broke up. . . ."

He really does mind about his parents' divorce, Spider told herself. The guy's human after all!

He shrugged, then finished, "Anyway, lo and behold, along came the gorgeous Joanna, and va-va-voom!"

"Oh," said Spider. Then, "So how come Mia got stuck with looking after me?"

"Nice assignment, huh? Oh, the Ice Queen's like that, even I have to give her credit. Big sense of duty—all that heavy stuff. Besides, she really likes Joanna."

Spider turned and stared at him. "How *can* she? When M . . . I mean, Joanna came along and married Andrew? If Mia really loves him, I mean?"

"Go figure," said Carter. "Nobility isn't my thing."

"Yeah, I can see that." Spider scrunched down in the seat. Wow, what a mess it all is, she thought. For everybody except the happy couple.

"What are *you* doing at the Dump anyway?" Carter asked, as he turned the car off the freeway and headed downtown.

"Surfing the Net," said Spider smugly.

"You musta had a brain transplant," said Carter. "Where do I turn next in this slum?"

"Uh, right at the light, I think."

Carter's car caused a minor sensation when it pulled up in front of the Dump. Jeers and catcalls filled the air.

A boy in a university jacket recognized Carter and yelled, "What are you doing down here, Craven? Slumming?"

Carter scowled. "I'll be back at ten," he muttered to Spider. "You better be ready."

"Or what?" Spider hopped out over the side of the car. "Your coach will turn into a pumpkin?" Whistles and a patter of applause greeted her.

"Picking them younger and younger, aren't you, Craven?" someone yelled out. "Can't you fool the big girls anymore?"

They fell about, laughing, as Carter roared away.

"Knock it off, coneheads. I'm his sister," said Spider, elbowing her way through the crowd.

Then thought: bite my tongue. What I just said!

Just as she got to the door, Jerry stuck his head out. "Thought I heard the welcome squad in action. C'mon up."

A strong smell made her wrinkle her nose as she tramped ahead of him up the narrow staircase to Cal's apartment. "Gee, what's that?" she asked over her shoulder.

Jerry grimaced. "Dinner. You were warned."

Cal greeted her like an old friend. He had an apron tied around his massive middle and was waving a wooden spoon.

"Can I . . . uh . . . help?" asked Spider, as Jerry took her jacket.

He rolled his eyes. "Too late!"

"Nonsense," bellowed Cal, who had ducked back into the kitchen. "Don't try to scare the poor girl off. You know you love my spaghetti, Jerry!"

Spider followed her nose to the kitchen with Jerry right behind her.

Cal grinned at her. He was stirring a cauldron of steaming water. A pot of sauce, the source of the peculiar smell, was bubbling away beside it. "Guess the spaghetti's about done," Cal said. "I threw some at the wall and it stuck."

"Is he kidding?" asked Spider, looking around just in case.

"Nope," replied Jerry, pulling a long face.

There was no spaghetti on the wall.

"Hope you like garlic," said Cal, beaming. "I use lots of it."

"I think Spider has figured that out for herself, Unk," said Jerry.

"Make yourself at home, Spider," said Cal, bustling around with plates.

Spider took in the scene. A small table had been carefully set for three, with spotless place mats and big, crisply ironed cloth napkins. There was even a pot of African violets in the middle.

Not bad, she told herself. In fact, pretty nice! Even Mia would approve.

Cal pulled out the chair at the middle place, and Spider sat down. Moments later a huge serving of spaghetti and meatballs was plunked down in front of her.

"Don't let it get cold," said Cal. "Jerry, pass the salad. And the garlic bread."

More garlic! Spider, who never ate it at home, sniffed suspiciously at the aromas wafting up from her plate.

Cal sat down and beamed across the table at Spider. "Well, this is what I like to see. It's about time Jerry brought a girl home to dinner."

Jerry blushed. "Aw, c'mon, Cal," he groaned.

Spider grinned. "No sweat," she told him. "Don't forget I've got one of them at home, too. Female version."

Jerry managed a feeble grin.

Despite the funny smell, everything tasted good.

"This is great, Cal," Spider said, digging in. She suddenly realized that she was starving.

"Don't let that go to your head, Unk," said Jerry. "Spider's pretty weird. Always has been."

"Gee, thanks," Spider shot back.

"Now that's something I wanted to ask you about," said Cal, pausing with his fork poised in midair. "How come you call this girl 'Spider'? And how come she lets you get away with it?"

Jerry looked stunned.

Spider shrugged. "It's not just Jerry," she said. "All the kids at school have called me Spider since grade three. When we moved here." She touched the spider mark. "You can see why. That, plus my last name."

"Which is?"

"Weber."

"Gotcha. Spider Weber. But that only answers one of my questions."

"You mean, why do I let them?" Spider asked. "Well, at first, because I couldn't stop them. Then I got used to it. Now I've kinda got to like it. It's different. Beats *Sara,* anyway."

Cal raised his eyebrows. "I don't agree," he said, primly. "Sara's a beautiful name. I'll call you Sara, if you don't mind."

"Be my guest," said Spider grandly.

Jerry grinned. "There's something you should know about the Unk. Under that Incredible Hulk exterior beats a heart of purest marshmallow. He used to wear daisies in his hair back in the sixties!"

"And was proud of it!" Cal insisted. "Back then people cared about things and let their feelings show. Our music did, too. Not like all the heavy metal garbage that passes for rock these days."

Jerry looked at Spider, and made a twirling motion with his finger beside his ear. *"Loco,* no?" he said. "Don't encourage him, Spider. He'll end up playing you his Joan Baez records and going all weepy on us!"

Cal sniffed disapprovingly. "You hard-boiled kids miss

out on a lot," he said with dignity. "There's no romance left in the world anymore." He flexed a massive bicep, making a heart-and-arrow tattoo bulge alarmingly.

Jerry and Spider snickered.

Jerry got up to clear away the plates. Cal pushed his chair back, and said, "Well, let's get down to it. I hear the joker has turned up again."

"Yeah," said Spider.

"And he said . . . ?"

"He said if I would just see him, he'd let me alone." Spider ran a fingernail back and forth on the table. "Do you think I should?"

Cal shook his head. "Uh-uh. No way. Not even in public, with other people around."

"Yeah, that's what I thought."

"I don't like this at all," mused Cal. "There's something going on we haven't figured out. I've nosed around a little. I know a guy at NetLink, and they can't believe it's one of their guys. My friend said that yours was the only account that had been tampered with. And Smiley didn't run up any bills or anything. Just read your mail and sent you those messages."

"You don't think he's just some smart-ass hacker, then?" asked Jerry.

"I did until now. Someone who gets off on breaking into systems, solving the problems just for the fun of it. And gets his jollies bugging people. Now I don't think so. So I did something I hope you don't mind my doing, Sara."

"What's that?"

"I called a buddy of mine on the city police force this afternoon. A junior detective. Les knows the Internet. Does a fair bit of surfing. I asked what the police attitude to all this would be."

"And?"

"Why not find out for yourself? I asked Les to drop by the Dump after supper."

Spider swallowed hard. "Gee. Yeah, well, I guess."

Cal glanced at his watch. "Should be here by now," he said.

"I'll check downstairs." Jerry got up and went out. A few minutes later he returned with a tall, slender black woman dressed in jeans, a leather jacket, and cowboy boots.

Spider's mouth dropped open. *"You're* the detective?"

"Uh-huh." She slung a leg over a chair and straddled it backwards.

"This is Sara, the girl with the smiley problem," said Cal, handing mugs of coffee around. "Sara, Detective Les Johnson, City Police."

Les raised her mug and sipped, smiling at Spider over the brim. She seemed friendly enough, but Spider felt as though she was being read by a laser scanner.

"Sara Craven, isn't it?" Les asked.

"No!" snapped Spider.

Les raised her eyebrows.

"Well, sort of," Spider admitted. "It's true my mother just married Andrew Craven. But my name is Weber. And it's gonna stay Weber."

"You don't sound too thrilled about your new stepfather," said Les.

Spider shrugged. "No one cares what I think."

"And your real father?"

"He's dead. He died when I was a baby."

"I see." Les put down her mug. "So what's goin' down?"

Cal filled her in on the whole situation.

"Mmmmm." Les considered. "The problem is that nothing criminal has occurred yet. Smiley hasn't threatened Sara, and he hasn't sent obscene messages."

Spider's heart sank. It was just what she'd expected the police would say. And it was true, after all. She couldn't explain to anyone why it all seemed as creepy to her as it did.

Les crossed her arms on the back of her chair and leaned her chin on them. Then, as if she'd been reading Spider's mind, she asked, "How do you feel about all this, Sara?"

Spider shivered. "Bad. Freaky."

Les slowly nodded her head. "Me, too," she said.

"Hey, really?" asked Jerry. "You don't think we're being dumb about this?"

"No way," Les replied. "It's a funny thing about my job. Most of it is strictly dealing with facts. You dig up the evidence, and when you've got enough, you get the picture."

"But . . . ?" prompted Cal.

"But there's something else a good detective needs. Intuition. A kind of feeling for when something's out of line. And my intuition is telling me that something is going on here. Don't know what, but something."

"Do you think it has something to do with Spider's being Andrew Craven's stepdaughter? I mean, someone trying to get at her because of who he is?"

"Could be. Someone as rich and famous as Craven attracts crazies the way a dog attracts fleas!"

"So what do I do?" asked Spider.

"For the moment, not much. Be careful. Don't go out alone anywhere, especially at night. Above all, don't agree to meet this guy. Not anytime, not anywhere. No matter what he says! Got it?"

Spider nodded. "Cal already told me that," she said.

"Okay," said Les. "Keep your eyes open, and let me know if you see anything, or if you get any more messages. I'm going to dig around a bit. Cal, you can help me with your Net connections."

Cal nodded.

"Oh . . . and Sara?" Les added.

"Yes?"

"Tell this Mia who's looking after you that something funny is going on. Right away. She has a right to know. She's responsible for you."

"I guess," said Spider. Great! she thought. If I tell Mia, she'll worm the whole story out of me. And she'll tell my mother—and Andrew—when they get back.

The thought of that really bugged her. What she did on

the Net was her business. She didn't want lectures from anybody!

"I want a firm yes on that, Sara," said Les, getting up. Her voice was soft, but the tone was steely.

Spider looked down at the table. "Yes," she mumbled.

"Good. Well, be seeing you all."

"Thanks a million, Les," Cal called after her. "I appreciate it."

"No sweat," said Les. She gave them a half-wave and disappeared down the stairs.

"That's one cool lady," said Cal, grinning.

> > >

He read the intranet message and swore under his breath. Craven was coming back sooner than expected. Some big takeover or other—no doubt more billions to be made.

They'd be back in just a couple of days. There was no time to waste if he wanted to get away with it. If only the kid had responded to his messages, it wouldn't be so hard on both of them now. And it *would* be hard, he knew that. Just for a moment, he hesitated. Should he let it go? Give up the whole idea and just leave town?

He rolled his shoulders, easing the tension in them, feeling the old familiar sense of anger and betrayal. No. He had waited long enough. He'd tried every other angle, and nothing had worked. This was the way it had to be. He had to go on, or what else was there for him?

His fingers played nervously over the keys, bringing up the plan of the house on-screen. His mind raced, calculating the simplest way to do it. It would be no sweat getting past the security system. He could see exactly how it was set up, and where the power and phone cables entered the house. There was just one real problem. The Par woman. Shouldn't be too hard to deal with her, though. He'd done some digging in her files, too, and he had an idea. All he needed now was a bit of luck.

Chapter 11

Spider was late getting up the next morning. She gulped her juice and ran, telling herself she'd keep her promise to get into the whole Smiley thing with Mia after school.

"Checked your e-mail yet?" Jerry whispered, as she dropped into her seat in front of him.

"Are you kidding? I haven't had time to breathe yet!"

"See you in the lab at lunchtime," he said.

At noon, they logged on to NetLink, and scrolled down the list of messages.

"Nothing," Spider said.

"That's good," he said. "Real good. Maybe give Cal and Les time to get on to something."

"Or maybe he'll just go away," said Spider, biting her lip.

"Don't count on it," said Jerry.

"Woo-woo, lovebirds!" It was Greg, making sucky kissing noises as he passed by on his way to a computer.

Spider snarled something at him that raised Jerry's eyebrows.

"Don't you think you're overdoing this flaming stuff?" he asked.

Spider shrugged. "Keeps coneheads like Greg off my back."

Jerry frowned. "I never understood why you were so scared of him. He's just a big jerk with a mean streak. From what I hear, his dad gives him a pretty hard time at home. I guess bullying other kids is the way he evens the score. You don't have to let him get to you."

"Believe me, I don't. Not any more," said Spider. She squirmed in her chair. Why should she care what grief Greg got at home, anyway?

"Yeah, but what about you?"

"What do you mean, what about me?"

"Do you really like being that way?"

"What way?"

"You know. Always swearing and bad-mouthing people."

"It's all an act, dummy. Some people think it's pretty cool." Spider wound a finger in her ponytail because she knew it bugged him.

Jerry rolled his eyes. "Yeah, well, don't get stuck in the role, if you get what I mean. Where I live I see plenty of tough cases around. Real ones. You don't need to act like one of them."

"You my keeper or something?" snapped Spider. "When I want your personal opinion, I'll ask for it!" Who did he think he was? Just because they were getting to be friends—sort of—that didn't give him the right to sound off at her.

"Ooookay!" Jerry shrugged and turned back to the computer.

Darn him anyway! she thought, as she clattered downstairs to her next class. Why did he always make her feel as if she was letting him down? Why should she even care? Well, she *didn't* care. She adjusted her backpack, and her swagger became strut. There was no way she was going to let any of this get to her—make her feel small again.

On the way home that afternoon, she again put off telling Mia about Smiley. After all, there'd be plenty of time if something else happened. Mia might just think she was being silly. But the excuse didn't sound convincing even to her. And what if Les found out somehow that she hadn't kept her word?

As usual, Mia's ESP was right on cue. She kept glancing at Spider as if she were waiting for her to say something. Spider even opened her mouth to tell her once, then closed it. It was all so embarrassing! By the time she'd got up her nerve, they were back at the house.

"I'm going grocery shopping," Mia announced. "Andrew and Joanna are due back, and I need to stock up. I'll be back in half an hour or so." She gave Spider a meaningful look. "It wouldn't hurt you to make a start on your homework," she hinted.

Blah, blah, blah, thought Spider, but she nodded.

Carter's Porsche was in the driveway again. The radio antenna was still extended, and she tweaked it as she passed. *Spoiinnng!*

She let herself into the house and walked over to the railing of the landing.

"Hey, Cementhead," she yelled. "You down there?" She thought she heard an answering growl from the kitchen.

She dumped her backpack in her room with a sigh. Putting off telling Mia hadn't made it any easier. She wished she'd got it over with.

She changed into jeans and a sweatshirt, and padded downstairs. The afternoon was closing in. The earlier sunlight was gone, and through the glass ceiling of the dining room she could see dark clouds building up.

Carter was in the kitchen, feet up on the table, reading a car magazine. With his blond hair, still wet from the shower, curling behind his ears, he looked more like a cover guy than ever.

He really is hunky, thought Spider. She could just imagine Lauren Pringle going into convulsions over Carter. Maybe she'd talk him into picking her up at school sometime, just for fun.

Carter glanced up. When he saw it was only Spider, he looked faintly relieved.

115

"On your own, Bugface?" he asked. "Where have you stashed your watchdog?"

"Mia's gone grocery shopping." Spider looked at her watch. "I wish she'd hurry up."

Carter raised his eyebrows. "You mean to say you actually want her around?"

"I have to talk to her about something," Spider said.

"Take my advice. Don't. When you talk to Mia you usually end up hearing something you don't want to hear." Carter returned to his magazine.

"You and she sure don't get along, do you?" asked Spider.

Carter gave her a cool stare. "Nosy, aren't you?" he asked.

Spider shrugged. "Just noticed. It's kind of hard to miss."

"Yeah, well, it's not exactly nuclear war. More of an armed truce. Mia doesn't go for anyone who gives Dad grief. And I'm the main contender. At least, since he and Mom split. Now, if you *really* want to see Mia get on someone's case, just ask her about DeeDee and the creepy guy she left Dad for. My *dear* stepfather, that is. The one who can't spend the money Dad gives Mom fast enough."

Yikes! Spider thought. No wonder Carter stayed at the frat house. He had problems wherever he went. Not that he didn't make plenty of them for himself.

"Thanks for the tip. I think I'll pass," she said. She dug a package of corn chips out of a cupboard, and told the Cat to turn on the TV.

"Weird, that," said Carter, looking up as a computer "painting" winked out and the Channel 9 logo appeared.

"Mmmmph?" Spider's mouth was full of corn chips.

"The Cat. How it lets you talk to it that way, when nobody else can."

Spider guzzled some cola, swallowed, and said, "Supposed to be a sort of present to me from your dad, Mia said."

"Must have taken him a lot of time to do that," said Carter. "And Dad doesn't have a lot of time. Tearing around the planet the way he does. He must really want to start out right with you, Bugface." He sounded puzzled.

"Oh, sure!" snapped Spider. But somehow she couldn't put the usual venom into it.

It was getting darker and darker, though it wasn't even five o'clock yet. The air felt strangely heavy. Spider got up and looked out the window at the woods all around. As she watched, a sudden breeze rippled the leaves, then just as suddenly died away. She turned back to the cheerful babble of the television.

A quarter of an hour later, Mia's car came down the road that led to the service entrance, and she appeared at the kitchen door with an armload of groceries. She dumped them on the table, then folded her arms, and stood looking down at Carter.

He ignored her for a moment, then looked up as though he had just noticed her arrival. "Oh, hi, Mia! You want something?" he asked innocently.

Mia jerked a thumb in the direction of the kitchen door. "There are more groceries. Lots of them. I had to stock up, especially with you eating your head off. So why not make yourself useful for a change?"

Carter muttered under his breath, but he got up and headed out to the car. Mia started putting groceries away. Spider went over and handed her things for the freezer.

Mia gave her a quick glance. "Everything okay, Sara?"

"Yeah. Well, there is something I need to talk to you about. Not really need. But maybe it's a good idea. Or maybe I should wait until Joanna gets back." Spider bit her lip. She was really making a mess of this.

"You might as well go ahead and tell me," prompted Mia. "Is it something to do with school?"

"No. It's the computer. At least that's how it started. . . ."

The phone rang, and Mia went over to answer it. "Craven residence, Mia Par speaking. Yes."

Thunder rumbled in the distance, and she raised her voice. "What? Who *is* this? How did you get this number?" she asked, frowning. "I asked who *is* this? What do you mean, my brother can't talk to me?"

Her hand clenched on the back of a chair, and she sat down slowly. "Which . . . which hospital? When was this? What . . . what do the doctors say?"

Carter ambled in with more groceries. He and Spider stood listening while Mia's voice became high and strained.

"No, I'm afraid I . . . Oh, no! Which hospital did you say? Yes. Yes, I understand." She hung up the phone and turned to Spider and Carter, her eyes brimming with tears.

"It's my brother. Carlito. He's been in a terrible accident. The hospital says I must go right away if . . . before . . ." She buried her face in her hands.

"Mia, you've got to go!" cried Spider.

"Do you need a ride?" Carter mumbled. "I mean, I could . . ."

Mia wiped her eyes "No. No, thank you, Carter. I don't know what to do. I don't like to leave you on your own, Sara. And I don't want to take you with me. Who knows when I'll get back? And you've got school tomorrow. . . ."

"For heaven's sake, get going!" urged Spider. "I'll be fine. Anyway, Carter's here now."

Mia reached for a tissue. "Will you . . . will you promise to stay right here till I get back, Carter?" she asked.

Carter shrugged. "I guess so."

Mia put her hand on his arm. "Please, Carter. This is important. Can I depend on you?"

Carter frowned and pulled his arm away. "Hey, don't you trust me, or what? I said I'd stay, didn't I?"

Mia looked abashed. "Sorry. Of course I trust you. All right, then. I'll try to get back later tonight, but I don't know if I can. The hospital he's in is a long way out of town. Anyway, I'll call you as soon as I get there. As soon as I know more." She picked up her handbag and went to the back door. Then she turned and said, "Thank you, Carter. I won't forget this." Moments later, her big, grey car sprayed gravel it as slewed around and disappeared back up the road.

Spider and Carter stared after it. Thunder growled again, much closer this time. Spider flinched. She'd been afraid of thunderstorms since she was a little kid. But there was no way she wanted Carter to know.

"Wow," said Carter. "I didn't know the Ice Queen had any feelings. Except about Dad."

"What a rotten thing to say," snapped Spider. "He's her kid brother, and she practically brought him up. Even I know that!"

"Hooray for you," said Carter. Then, "I knew it would come down to this one of these days," he added glumly. "Baby-sitting."

"Yeah," Spider shot back. "Me baby-sitting you!"

"Swell," said Carter. He sat down at the kitchen table and folded his arms. "So what's for supper?"

"You paralyzed or something?"

"Something," he said, grinning.

Spider blew her bangs up from her forehead. "Oh, for cripes' sake!" She started unpacking the rest of the groceries. Then, "Saved!" she exclaimed a moment later. "She bought frozen pizza."

"It'll do," said Carter, reaching for his magazine.

Spider shoved the box across the table. "Oh, no you don't! You fix the pizza while I put the rest of this stuff away. All you have to do is heat the oven and put it in. Just don't forget to take the wrapper off."

"Very funny." But he checked the package and got up to set the oven.

By the time they had finished eating, the storm had broken. Wind lashed the trees along the ravine, and lightning flickered all around them. Then rain began to fall, first a few big drops splattering against the windows, then torrents.

Carter got up and stretched. "Well, it's been a blast, Bug-face. Thanks for the chow," he said. "Even if I did have to cook it myself. Guess I'll be pushing off."

"P . . . pushing off?" stammered Spider. "But you're supposed to stay! Mia said . . . and you promised!"

"Sure. Sure I did. I mean, she had to go, right? And that was the only way to make her. But that doesn't mean I actually have to stay, does it? After all, I'm a big boy now. I do what I want. And *only* what I want."

He headed for the stairs.

"Why would you want to go out in weather like this, anyway?" Spider yelled after him.

"'Cause I've got plans for the evening." he shouted back. "And don't ask me what, because I won't tell you."

Spider bounded up the stairs after him, flinching again as lightning flashed almost overhead. The house had so much glass that it was almost like being outside in the storm.

She caught up with him on the landing. "Uh, Carter, can I come with you?" she asked, hoping it didn't sound too much like begging.

Carter stopped dead with one arm into his windbreaker. "You kidding or something, Bugface? A kid like you hanging out with me? The places I go? My dad would boil me in oil if he ever found out. That is, if Mia didn't skin me alive first!"

"Then couldn't you drop me off at the Dump?" pleaded Spider. "Cal and Jerry wouldn't mind."

Carter turned up his jacket collar and pulled out his car keys. "What's this all about, kid? I know you're weird, but not so weird that you're scared to stay home alone."

"It's just . . . just, well, I've been getting some weird messages on my e-mail. . . ." Spider began.

Carter's eyes narrowed. "Don't get into all that garbage with me, okay? That's Dad's kind of stuff—he's always on my case about it! If you get off on being a cyberjerk, too, bully for you! You, he, and Joanna can be a happy little trio. I just don't want to hear anything about it!" he snapped.

Then, seeing the worry on her face, he put a hand on her shoulder and gave her a little shake. "Now look, Bugface. You're an okay kid. Kinda spooky, but you'll do. Just don't get in my face, okay?" He ran his hand through his hair. "Look, you'll be fine here on your own," he went on. "The house has more security systems than the national mint. You're totally safe here, believe me. And I'll be back later. A *lot* later, but I'll definitely come back."

"I know," Spider mumbled. "But . . ."

"And remember, you owe me one," he added. "We agreed on it, didn't we? So be a good girl and don't make a fuss. And don't rat to Mia, either."

"I wouldn't rat!" said Spider, bristling. "Not even on a creep like you!"

"Atta girl!" Carter opened the door, and a gust of wind laced with rain roared in. "See you later," he called and made a dash for his car.

Spider slammed the door and heard the automatic dead bolt click into place. She wrapped her arms around herself and shivered. What was the matter with her, anyway? Why was she so jumpy? She felt as though she had shrunk, as though her skin were suddenly too big for her.

It was just that the house felt big and empty, she told herself. It would be good to talk to Cal or Jerry.

She walked along the hall to the Treehouse and picked up the phone. She keyed in the number of the Dump, but the line was busy. So she flicked on the computer and told the Cat to take her to NetLink.

There was a message from Cal in her e-mail.

From: Cal@hexdump.com
We think we're on to something. Smiley's gotta be someone working from inside Craven Corporation. It's the only way he could get all the information he's been showing off. Les has asked the company to check into their employees' online records. Sit tight.
Cal

Right below it was another smiley.

From: smiley@rin.com
Your friends think they're pretty smart, don't they? It won't do them any good to check up on me—I've covered my tracks. Anyway, it doesn't matter now. I can't wait anymore, Sara. I'll be seeing you soon.
:=)

Be seeing you! Spider shivered. She clicked on Prepare and began typing.

To: cal@hexdump.org
Cal, Jerry. Another smiley. He knows you're checking him out at Craven Corp. Says he'll be seeing me soon. Can't reach you by phone. Hope you get this right away! I'm alone at the house. Please come!
spider

She sent the e-mail, then tried the phone again. Still busy. She'd just have to keep trying. No telling when Cal or Jerry would check the Dump's e-mail.

She walked back to the landing and stood staring down over the railing at the lighted levels below her. The house felt like a huge ship, its prow riding the storm. Everything was warm and glowing. Soft lights, bright colors, warm air with just the trace of a breeze stirring. The Cat had everything under control.

Carter was right, she told herself. There was nothing to be afraid of. No matter what kind of a troublemaker Smiley was, she was safe. All she had to do was sit tight. . . .

A brilliant flare of lighting lit the wild scene outside for an instant, then came a crack of thunder so loud that Spider clapped her hands over her ears.

Moments later, the house died. The lights went out, and the purr of the air conditioning stopped. There was a moment of eerie silence before the next roll of thunder rattled the windows.

"Please, God," prayed Spider.

A long moment passed. She tried to be calm and think what to do. Slowly, her mind focused. Mia had said that the house had its own generator. The Cat must be able to control the emergency power. That was it! All she had to do was find a remote or get to one of the Cat's Ears.

Then, gradually, the lights came back on. Air moved and the computer image-paintings on the walls sprang to life again.

Spider took a deep breath. She should have known. The Cat must have a default setting to turn on the emergency generator automatically after a power cut. She giggled. "Attaboy, Cat!" she said into the Cat's Ear near the head of the west stairs.

Purrrr! went the air conditioning. She pattered downstairs through the glass-walled galleria, crossed the dining room, and went into the kitchen. Funny, after her scare she felt hungry again. The storm was passing, the thunder grumbling away into the distance. Rain was sheeting down, and the stream, swollen by the runoff, roared as it plunged down into the ravine below.

What a dork she had been to be so spooked! Carter was a rat, but he was right about one thing. There was nowhere safer than Fallingbrook. And with any luck, Cal or Jerry would get her message and come over.

Spider pulled off a doughy wedge of cold pizza and stood there, chewing. Anchovy and pepperoni was her favorite, hot or cold. She turned and reached into the fridge for a pop, then froze in the act, her eye caught by something on the floor inside the kitchen door.

Between the doorway and the mat was a large, wet footprint.

Spider's stomach hit her ribs. She wasn't alone in the house!

Chapter 12

Her mind slammed into overdrive. She reached the wall phone in a single bound and yanked off the receiver. The line was dead. Then she thought of the cell phone. That would still work! She spun around, eagerly, but it was nowhere in sight. Then she remembered having seen it upstairs somewhere. The hall table?

Maybe she could get to it. But where was the intruder? Not in the galleria or the dining room—she'd just come from there. He must have gone upstairs, taking the kitchen staircase as she came down the galleria.

Should she take off out the back door? She was at the bottom of the ravine, and the service road wound for a kilometer through dense woods before emerging on a back road. And maybe there were more prowlers outside.

Better to grab the phone and get out the front door if she could. From the top of the ravine, Riverside Drive was only a few hundred meters away. She could phone for help, and there were houses, buses, traffic. She turned back toward the dining room, then hesitated. No, it was too open. It would be too easy for him to see her from the top of the house. And he'd already been up the kitchen stairs—he might be coming down the galleria right now!

She swallowed hard and began edging up the kitchen stairs that led to the living room on the level above. She crouched down when she neared the top and peered into the room. Nothing. She could see a bit of the railing of the landing above. Nothing there, either. She waited, listening for the least sound that would give the intruder away.

Silently, she cursed the roar of the rain and the thunder of the stream. They made it hard for her to hear.

Then she did hear something, or thought she did. A muffled thud from the direction of the galleria stairs. He must have gone back down there looking for her.

Hope leaped up inside her. If she could just get across the living room and up the main stairs, she might make it!

She was halfway across when something told her to look up.

And there he was. Tall, thin, dressed in black sweats and a windbreaker, he was standing just behind the railing of the landing looking down at her.

"Hi, Sara," he said, softly. "Don't be scared. I don't want to frighten you, but this seems to be the only way I can get to see you."

"Smiley?" Spider croaked, her voice breaking on a high note of terror. He didn't look like the kind of nightmare figure she'd been imagining, but there was an intensity about him, a kind of crackling suppressed energy. "But I heard . . ."

He took a small polished stone from a tray of river rocks on the table beside him, and tossed it gently down to the level below. It landed on the carpet with a muffled thud. The thud she had heard.

"What . . . what do you want?" stammered Spider. As long as he didn't come any closer she could go on breathing.

"Just to talk to you. I keep telling you that. And I hope I can persuade you to spend some time with me. I won't hurt you, Sara, believe me. I want to be your friend."

Friend!

"T . . . talk about what? The Internet?"

"Oh, no. Not about that. Though you were pretty silly to do some of the things you did, weren't you, Sara? You were getting a bit out of control. I got quite worried about you."

"I'm sorry. I . . . I won't ever do stupid stuff like that again," said Spider.

Smiley nodded. "No, of course you won't," he said. "People do foolish things when they're unhappy, don't they? I bet you've been plenty unhappy lately. With your mother getting married and all. I saw their picture in the paper, and I didn't feel too happy myself." He drew a deep breath. "Well, that's the past, isn't it? Once you and I get to know one another better, I know we'll both be a lot happier. Wait a minute and I'll come down." He started for the stairs.

Spider began backing away. If she could make it down the kitchen stairs and out the door maybe she could hide in the woods.

"Sara!" Something pleading in the tone of his voice made Spider look back.

Smiley had stopped where he was. "There's no need to run away," he coaxed. "Won't you just stop and listen to me for a few minutes? Then you won't want to run away. I won't come any closer if you don't want me to, I promise."

"Who are you?" Spider cried. "What do you want?"

"My name is Carl Weber, Sara. I'm your father."

Spider froze. "That's crazy. You're crazy! I don't have a father. He's dead. He died when I was a baby!"

Smiley winced as if her words had struck him. Then he said, "I was afraid Joanna might have told you something like that. I hoped she hadn't. But it must have made things so much simpler for her."

Spider stared at him for a long moment, then burst out, "I don't believe you!"

"Your name is Sara Louise Weber. Your birthday is January 23, and you were born at Centennial Hospital in Toronto. I was there. You weighed seven pounds, five ounces. You had a lot of dark hair and a mole on your right knee."

Spider shook her head. "Oh, no. Oh no, you don't, Mister. You can't fool me. You could find out every bit of that stuff through computers. You're so darn smart at that, aren't you?" Angrily, she tipped up her chin and pointed at her spider mark. "Well, take a look at this! What about my birthmark? You didn't know about that, did you? You aren't my father!"

"I know all about that," Smiley replied quietly. "And I really am your father. You can ask Joanna. She'll tell you the truth now. She'll have to."

Had her mother lied to her? Lied all her life? She couldn't have! Could she? But . . . wasn't there something familiar about Smiley's bony, peaky face? Didn't she see something very like it in the mirror every morning?

Spider shivered and felt the prickle of tears down her face.

Then Smiley started down the stairs toward her.

She whirled and ran for the kitchen stairs.

"Don't run, Sara," she heard him call out. "Please don't!"

Ignoring him, she raced across the kitchen and tried to wrench the outer door open. It wouldn't budge.

Stupid! she cursed herself. The lock's on! She heard Smiley running lightly down the stairs behind her.

Too late! She'd never make it.

She spun around and ran out into the dining room, putting the huge wooden refectory table between them.

"Sara, this is silly," Smiley said, stopping at the end of the table, while Sara backed slowly toward the other end. "Don't make me chase you like this."

"Then get out!" screamed Sara. "Just get out and leave me alone!"

"I can't do that," Smiley said quietly. "I've had to leave you alone all these years, haven't I? It wasn't supposed to be that way. I was supposed to be able to visit you. But the two of you just disappeared. I've tried and tried to find you, but I didn't know where you were until just recently. When your mother got engaged to Craven."

"But . . . but how did you know where we live? Nothing

like that is ever published about Andrew. And the phone's unlisted!"

He shrugged. "I got a job at Craven International."

So Cal and Les were right!

"All I had to do was hack into Craven's personal files to find your address," Smiley went on. "And a whole lot more."

Spider backed away.

"Listen, Sara," said Smiley. "I keep telling you I won't hurt you. You're my daughter. All I want is to get to know you. Isn't that a fair thing to ask? Joanna's had you to herself all these years. Now it's my turn—though she never intended me to have a turn. Won't you come and live with me for a while? Once we're safely away we can let your mother know. Anyway, she doesn't really need you now, does she? She's got Craven and all his billions." He started around the end of the table.

Spider glanced at the galleria stairs. They were still too far away for her to make a dash for them. She had to get closer. . . .

Suddenly Smiley's temper flared, and he smacked his hand hard on the table. "Dammit, Sara. Stop trying to run away! Haven't you listened to a word I've said? Talk to me. Say something!"

"Uh, how did you get in?" asked Spider shakily, taking another step backwards.

"What does that matter?" he asked impatiently. "It's easy enough if you know how. The house plans are right there in Craven's file, showing where the power and phone lines come in. It was easy to figure out how to cut them. The plans also showed exactly how the emergency default system works. I knew it would take a minute to respond to a power loss. So after I cut the power, I just opened the door and walked in."

"So it was *you*, not the storm at all!" Spider breathed.

He nodded his head. "That's right."

"But how . . . how did you know I'd be alone?" Another

small step backwards, one foot sliding behind the other.

"I knew the Par woman would be here. Everyone at Craven knew she was looking after you. But my fake phone call took care of her." Smiley shrugged. "The only glitch was Craven's son. He hasn't been around much, so I hadn't counted on his being in the house. I've been watching the place, and I almost gave up when I saw his car in the driveway. But I decided to hang around, just in case. It was my last chance, you see. Craven and Joanna are on their way home. So it was a real stroke of luck for me when he took off. I waited awhile to be sure he wasn't coming back, then I cut the power."

He came around the edge of the table. Spider backed up. Then she turned and ran for the galleria.

"Sara, please!" he shouted.

She raced up the stairs, but she could hear Smiley behind her. She knew she'd never make it to the front door. Somehow, she had to gain some time.

"Wait, stop! Don't chase me!" she yelled. "I'll never go with you if you chase me!" She reached the second set of stairs and ran up them, then took a chance and glanced back.

He had stopped at the top of the first set of stairs.

Spider leaned against the wall, panting. "You're scaring me," she called down, shakily. "If you were really my father you wouldn't want to scare me."

Smiley held out his hands palms upward. "Believe me, Sara. I *am* your father, and I don't want to scare you. But I've waited so long to see you. And now there's not much time. You've got to come with me before someone shows up and stops us. Joanna will never let you be with me. If she were willing to share you, she wouldn't have lied about me, would she?"

"Where . . . where would we go?" Spider eased backwards along the wall.

"First to my apartment. We'll have to get out of town fast, though. The city will be crawling with police once they find out you're missing. But don't worry. We'll get a swell new place soon. I can get a computer job anywhere, make lots of money. You can have anything you want."

Spider kept edging backwards. Somehow she had to distract him. Or delay him. Her mind worked furiously. There must be computer controls for the galleria, she knew. Lights. Art. Doors . . . *Doors!*

There were sliding doors at both ends of the passage. If she could get out before him and close them. . . . But she had no remote. Would the Cat . . . ? There was a Cat's Ear on the upper landing. If she could reach it in time, it might work. It was her only chance.

"Okay . . . Dad," she said slowly, the word bitter on her tongue. "If you really want me to come, I'll do it. But I'll have to leave a message for Mom, so she'll know I'm all right."

His thin face lit up. "Oh, Sara, it's going to be great," he said eagerly. "Just the two of us—at least for a while. You'll see." He started up the stairs, more slowly now.

"Just let me get a few things from my room—and write the note," she called down to him as she turned and bounded up the last set of stairs.

He was still on the second level when she reached the upper landing.

"Cat! Shut the galleria doors!" she screamed into the Cat's Ear. Instantly, the doors slid silently out of the wall and moved across, sealing the passage at both ends.

As she ran across the landing, she could hear him pounding on the doors, yelling, "Sara, come back! *Sara!*"

She knew she hadn't gained much time. He'd figure out how to disable the doors, force them apart, get at the electric wires or something. She had to reach the street quickly. Had to!

In her panic, she forgot the cell phone. "Unlock the front door!" she yelled, praying the Cat could pick up her words from across the landing. She heard the dead bolt click back. Whimpering with fear, she wrenched the door open and ran out into the rain, her feet digging deep into the wet gravel as she tried to pick up speed. It was like running in a nightmare, getting nowhere.

She slipped on the gravel and went down on one knee. Gasping for breath, she glanced back over her shoulder at the house and saw Smiley silhouetted for a moment against the light spilling out of the doorway. He'd freed himself already! Sobbing, she got to her feet and struggled on.

Then she ran straight into someone.

For a moment she thought she'd die of fright. Then she recognized who it was. "Cal!" she sobbed, throwing her arms around his bulky body. "Oh, Cal, it's Smiley! He's here!"

Looking up, she saw Jerry peering at her over Cal's shoulder, his face dead white and scared.

"Yeah," growled Cal. "We got your message. Looks like Les is taking care of him pretty good."

Spider looked back. Les had Smiley face down on the gravel, and had pinioned his arms behind him. As Spider watched, she pulled out a pair of handcuffs and snapped them on his wrists.

Cal turned her around and held her back from him by both shoulders. "Sara, did he hurt you?" he asked gently.

Jerry peeled off his jeans jacket and wrapped it around her. Spider snuggled into it, shivering. His arm felt good around her shoulder.

"No," gasped Spider. She pushed her sopping wet hair out of her eyes. "No. He . . . he says he's my father. He wanted to take me away."

"Your father!" rumbled Cal.

"You told us he was dead!" said Jerry, staring at her wide-eyed.

"I thought he was! My mother always said he died when I was just one year old. He says she lied. . . ."

Distant sirens grew closer, then headlights swept the driveway as two police cars roared up, their red lights whirling. Spider shielded her eyes against the glare.

"The girl's okay! Detective Johnson's got the guy," yelled

Cal, pointing, as two police officers dashed past them.

A couple of minutes later, Les and the others came back pushing Smiley none too gently ahead of them.

Smiley stopped for a moment in front of Spider. His face was streaked with mud, and there was a gash from the gravel on one cheek. "Sara . . . I'm sorry," he said. "I didn't want it to happen this way. I really didn't mean to scare you. And I wouldn't ever hurt you. Please believe me. "

Spider gulped down a sob. She stood staring after him as the police led him to one of the prowl cars. Tears and rain were running down her face.

She wished she could run and keep on running. Away from all of it. From all of them. Because somehow she knew that everything Smiley had told her was true.

Chapter 13

The detective inspector was frowning. "You mean after that guy broke in here the other night and terrorized your stepdaughter, you're not going to press charges?" he asked, raising his bushy eyebrows.

There were just the three of them sitting with Les and the inspector in the living room. Mia had gone home, and Carter had vanished into thin air.

Joanna and Andrew had arrived back the day after the break-in to find a police guard at the gate, Spider hiding out in her room, and Mia in tears. Carter nowhere to be found. Spider had said almost nothing to her mother since. How could she say, "You lied to me?" But if she didn't, what *could* she say to her? Ever.

Now Andrew turned to Spider. "It's your call, Sara, " he said, his face solemn. "Are you sure that's still the way you want it?"

Joanna started to say something, but Andrew shook his head, and she fell silent.

Spider nodded. She glanced at her mother, who was frowning, then looked away. She knew Joanna didn't like her decision, but Andrew had said it was up to her to choose, and so she had.

She'd thought about it and thought about it, and now she was sure. Smiley had frightened her, all right. And he shouldn't have come after her that way. But he hadn't hurt her, hadn't meant to. And now that she knew, how could she send her own father to jail?

"But let's make that conditional on his getting professional help," Andrew said to the inspector. "The guy's obviously got problems. And he has to agree to stay away from Sara."

"Absolutely," Joanna cut in.

"Shouldn't be too difficult to get some kind of a restraining order from the court," said Les, smiling at Spider. "And we'll keep an eye on him for a while to make sure he obeys it. And Sara, if he tries to contact you again by e-mail, you'll let us know right away, promise?"

"I promise," said Spider.

"That about wraps it up, then," said the inspector.

"Uh, can I ask something?" Spider said quickly.

"Go ahead."

"How come you guys showed up when you did? I mean, Cal and Les got my e-mail, but how . . . ?"

"Easy. I called the station on my cell phone," Les said, grinning. "Cal and I spotted a car parked in the woods near the front gate and thought we'd better have help."

"Oh," said Spider.

"Funny thing, though," the inspector said. "We were already on our way. Because we got another call first."

"Who from?" Spider and Les spoke at once.

"Guess it's a *what*, not a *who*," replied the inspector. "It was some weird kind of computer security system. Called itself HouseCat. It said you had a prowler who had tampered with the house systems."

Everyone looked at Andrew.

"Well, yes," he admitted, looking sheepish. "I programmed it to do that."

"Thank God," breathed Joanna.

"Yaaay, Cat!" said Spider.

After the police had gone, Andrew looked from Spider to Joanna. "I think you'd better get on with it, Jo," he said, resting his hand on her shoulder for a moment. Then he turned and went downstairs, leaving them together.

Spider didn't know what to say, so she said nothing.

After a moment, Joanna said, "I need a breath of fresh air. Do you mind if we talk outside?"

She sounds so formal, thought Spider. As if she's talking to a grown-up. Was her mother feeling as strange about it all as she was?

They went out through the French doors that led off the landing to a small patio overlooking the stream.

For a few moments they stood listening to the water. Then, *"Why?"* Spider asked. She struggled to keep the anger out of her voice, to make it sound like a neutral question. "Why did you lie to me about my father?"

Her mother sighed. "Oh, Sara, it was all kinds of reasons, really. When you were little, it just seemed right. It was easy to tell you that your daddy had died. It saved so many questions—questions I didn't want to answer."

Spider just gazed at her, and after a moment Joanna went on. "And as you got older, I just couldn't bring myself to tell you the truth."

She clasped her hands together and pressed them against her lips. After a moment, she went on, "I told myself I was thinking only of you, of course. But I guess I was really just as much concerned for myself. My pride. What you would think of me if I told you I'd lied. And maybe not telling you the truth was a way of blocking out bad memories, too."

"Please. I need to know about it. Whatever it was," Spider spoke stiffly, not wanting to beg.

"Yes. I know you do, hon." Joanna shivered and wrapped her sweater more closely around her shoulders. "But I can hardly bring myself to talk about it, even now." She took a deep breath. Then, "Your father used to hit me, Sara. Sometimes, when he got angry," she said.

"Hit you? *You?*" said Spider. She couldn't imagine her

mother taking anything from anybody. She was always the big boss, the one in charge.

"Thanks for the implied compliment," said Joanna. "Oh, Carl wasn't always that way. But whenever things got tough, and he didn't get the jobs or the money he wanted . . . thought he deserved, he'd take it out on me. He has a short fuse. Maybe you saw a bit of that the other night."

Spider nodded slowly, remembering the way his anger had flared up as she ran away from him.

"And . . . and here's the really awful part." Joanna's voice quivered, then steadied. "I let it go on, Sara! For five years! I think I even blamed myself in some crazy way. Thought that if I had been a better wife, instead of an ignorant, une-ducated girl, he would have loved me more. That was non-sense, of course."

Spider felt the icy edge of her anger beginning to melt. Her mother looked smaller, somehow. Like someone recov-ering from a long illness. Spider still wanted answers, but was afraid there was no way to ask the questions. "You . . . you don't have to talk about it if it bothers you too much," she said slowly.

Joanna reached out and pressed her hand against Spider's cheek. "Thanks. But I think it's better if I tell you everything now I've begun. Then you can make up your own mind about . . . all of it. After all, you're almost a grown-up now. Funny how I keep forgetting that. It's time I stopped hiding things."

After a moment she went on. "It was already pretty bad before I had you."

Suddenly, Joanna's eyes brimmed with tears. "Gosh, I was so thrilled about you, Sara. I was ecstatic," she went on, meeting Spider's gaze. "About you, yourself, most of all. But I guess I also thought having you would fix everything that was wrong between your father and me, too. Of course it didn't."

"He . . . he didn't want me," said Spider, her mouth dry.

"Oh, he did," said Joanna. "He was proud of you, Sara. I

won't lie about that to you. But having a small baby and not much money made life more difficult, and he couldn't always handle that."

"He went on hitting you?"

Joanna nodded. "Sometimes. And one night, well, I was cooking supper. We argued. He started yelling at me. Something just . . . snapped in me, and I started yelling back. It was our worst quarrel ever. I was standing at the stove, heating oil in a frying pan. Carl jerked the pan out of my hand and slammed it down, hard. It bounced off the stove. I jumped back and knocked your high chair over, and Sara . . . oh, Sara, some of the oil hit you. Burned into your little face. You started screaming. . . ." Joanna buried her face in her hands.

Numbly, Spider touched the mark on her cheek. After a moment she said, "So it isn't a birthmark at all. It's a scar." Then she remembered. "He said he knew all about it," she added.

"Yes," said Joanna wearily. "Oh, Carl was terribly upset by what he'd done. Took us to the hospital. Promised he'd never lose control again. But how could I believe him? For me it was the end. As soon as he went to work the next day, I took you and ran. I kept running all the way down East. Found a job. Signed up for night school. Started over."

A sudden thought struck Spider. "Did . . . did you ever get divorced from him?" she whispered.

Joanna gave her a lopsided smile. "Poor Sara! Do you think I'm a bigamist, too? Don't worry—we did get divorced. Two years later. It was all done through lawyers, and Carl went along with it. Out of guilt, I guess. Anyway, I never saw him again. And the moment it was done, just to be sure, I moved again and left no forwarding address. And then later we came way out here to the Coast."

She shivered. "I got a bad feeling when the papers ran my picture with Andrew's. But I told myself I was being silly. So many years had gone by, and Carl had never come after us. I thought we were safe. And I never dreamed he'd try to take you!"

"He . . . he said he wanted to get to know me," faltered Spider. "He said you've cheated him of something, something he had a right to. And wanted me to get to know him, too."

Joanna sighed. "Yes, I can see how he would feel that way. Maybe I should have handled things differently. But at the time I just . . . couldn't."

There was a pause. Then she went on, "Sara . . . I can't bear to think that you might not trust me now. I'll never lie to you again, I swear it! Can you forgive me?"

Could she?

Spider knew she had to say something, but couldn't find the words. *Can* I trust her? she wondered. Then, yes. Always to do what she thinks is best for me. But she might not always be right. Like lying to me about Smiley. Dad. So . . . so I'll have to figure out what's right for myself, won't I?

The silence between them grew long, and then at last Spider said slowly, "It's . . . it'll be all right . . . Mom." She put her arms around her mother.

They were still standing that way when the glass doors slid open behind them, and Andrew peered out. Spider suddenly noticed that he, too, looked worn out, older somehow. Could it be because of what had happened to her? That he really did care about her?

Joanna's weary face lit up, and she held out both hands to him.

She really loves Supernerd, Spider thought. Amazing!

"Did you tell her?" he asked Joanna. "Everything?"

Joanna nodded.

"You mean you knew? She told *you?*" demanded Spider, glaring at Andrew. How could her mother have told this terrible stuff to him when she wouldn't trust her own daughter!

"Yes," Joanna said quickly, putting her hand on Spider's arm. "Sara, I couldn't marry him unless he knew about my past. And you know what? Right from the beginning he said I had to tell you the truth about Carl. And I was going to do it. Truly I was."

"Oh." Spider felt deflated.

Andrew shuffled his feet and cleared his throat. "Uh, Sara?" he asked.

"Yeah?" Her chin went up. How could she talk to him about any of this? After all, she hardly knew the guy!

"About Mia," he began, frowning.

Mia had left that morning, and Spider had helped her carry her stuff out to her car. She'd leaned in the passenger window to take a last sniff of the leather upholstery. "Hey, guess I'm gonna miss . . ." she began, then paused for a beat, and finished, "the classy car."

Mia had managed a smile. "Oh, I'll be around sometimes," she said. "When I've . . . got used to things." Then she added, "I will, you know. And so will you." For a moment their eyes met.

"Yeah, I guess," Spider mumbled. She stepped back and jammed her hands in her pockets.

Mia slid on her huge sunglasses and started the engine. Then she looked across at Spider and asked, "How about coming downtown and having lunch with me sometime?"

Spider grinned. "Hey! At the top of the Tower?"

"Right at the very top," promised Mia.

"Can I wear my Docs?" Spider asked slyly.

Mia shuddered. "If you absolutely must!"

Spider waved as the big grey car sped away down the drive.

Now she hurried to make Andrew understand. She couldn't bear for him to be angry with Mia. Not when, not when . . .

"You mustn't blame Mia. Not for anything," she told him. "There was no way Mia could have guessed what was going on. Les—Detective Johnson—made me promise to tell her, but I didn't. Then my . . . Smiley made up that fake phone call to fool her. And she thought I'd be safe with Carter here."

Andrew's expression became grim. Spider had never seen him look this way—cold and hard. She was suddenly very glad he wasn't angry at her.

"Ah, yes, Carter," said Andrew. "There's no excuse for what he did, Sara. Leaving you like that after he'd promised Mia he'd stay." Then he shook his head, and some of the anger went out of his face. "I want you to know that I've had it out with him. But I guess I have to blame myself, too. He's been a problem since he was a little kid. Maybe it was me. Maybe I didn't take enough time to be with him when he needed me. Then his mother and I divorced, and I left him to her, more or less. Now he doesn't want any part of me—except my money. And he hates everything I stand for. I just can't seem to reach him."

To her amazement, Spider heard herself saying, "Carter can be a real stinker. But . . . but maybe he thinks nobody cares about him."

Andrew raised his eyebrows. "You know, he told me almost the same thing himself. And I'm going to try to do something about that, but still . . ."

Spider rushed on, "And after all, Carter didn't know what was going on any more than Mia did. I hadn't told anybody but Jerry and Cal."

Andrew nodded. "Speaking of those two . . ."

"The Geek and the Unk," said Spider. "I owe them a lot."

Andrew smiled, and Spider noticed he looked a lot less nerdy that way.

"We all do. I was on the phone to Cal first thing this morning," he said. "To say a heartfelt thanks. And to tell him that when the time comes, Jerry has a scholarship to any university he chooses. Anywhere in the world. All expenses paid. As for Cal, he'll be getting new computers for the Dump. Top of the line. As many as he wants. And upgrades forever."

Spider grinned at him. "Jerry will think he's died and gone to heaven. He's always beefing about the old dinosaurs they have."

Andrew's face grew serious again, and he said, "One last thing. After what happened, I'm sure you won't want to go on living here. I just wanted to let you know I'll be putting the house up for sale as soon as we can find somewhere else to live."

"Sell Fallingbrook?" Spider was stunned. "But you'd be selling the Cat!"

Andrew shrugged. "HouseCat will have to be deprogrammed."

But that would kill it! Spider opened her mouth to tell him he mustn't, then closed it. It would sound so stupid. But the Cat seemed so real!

"I can rebuild something like it somewhere else," Andrew went on. "But maybe I won't—not that way. I guess I've meddled in your life more than enough, Sara. Cueing the Cat to your voice prompts, I mean." He pushed up his cloudy glasses, which had slid down his nose. "I got so excited figuring out how to do it that I didn't stop to think you mightn't like it. Sorry about that. I've always been a whiz with computers, but I guess I'm not with people."

Carter said that, too, thought Spider. Then another thought struck her, and she stared blankly at Andrew. *He* was the Cat! Its smart talk, its purrs and whispers, its ridiculous grin—all of that came from Andrew. He'd made her a kind of goofy gift of himself.

And none of what had happened was really his fault. She and her mother had brought their trouble with them.

"Aw, I dunno," she mumbled. "The Cat's pretty weird, but I've kind of got used to it." On impulse, she reached out and lifted off Andrew's glasses. She wiped them clean on the bottom of her sweatshirt, then set them back on his nose.

Andrew beamed. "Thanks," he said. "I needed that." Then he added, "About the house, though. Maybe you should think about it some more?"

Spider shrugged. "Okay," she said. It wouldn't hurt him to wait a bit, she told herself, but deep down she knew they'd be staying.

Spider left her mother and Andrew in the living room. They kept looking at each other in a mushy kind of way,

141

and she couldn't handle too much of that. At least not yet, she told herself, thinking of Mia.

She climbed the stairs and padded along to the Treehouse. The phone was ringing, and she ran to pick it up, figuring it would be Cal or Jerry.

"Hello?" she said eagerly.

A voice said, "That you, uh . . . Sara?"

"Carter?"

"Yeah." There was a pause, then he said, "Uh, about what happened. Like, Dad told me all the details. Tore a real strip off me for leaving you alone like that."

"Mmm." Spider twirled the phone cord, wondering what was coming next.

"Jeez, I'm sorry, kid. Real sorry," Carter mumbled. "I mean, how was I to know some maniac could break into the house?"

"That maniac is my father," said Spider. Then realized how peculiar that sounded.

"Yeah, well . . ." Carter's voice trailed off. "Anyway, guess I'll be seeing you around. Dad has laid down the law. I have to live with you guys from now on. Or it's no allowance for me."

"Wow! No more Porsches unless you behave. Guess he cares about you after all, huh?"

There was a grunt from the other end of the line.

"Well, you sure don't sound too thrilled about it!" Spider prodded.

"Nah. Who wants to hang out with a couple of dewy-eyed newlyweds and a brat?" growled Carter.

"Loooove you toooo, Rock Ears," cooed Spider.

Carter chuckled. "Catch ya later, kid."

She put down the receiver and stood looking at the phone for a minute. Then she shook her head. "Weirder and weirder," she muttered.

Restless, she wandered out onto the deck, the door sliding back smoothly ahead of her. The wind was up, and the sun was setting over the woods. Spider shaded her eyes, watching the racing clouds.

Funny how you could sometimes see shapes in clouds as clear as clear, and then they changed. It was sort of the same with people. Nobody was really the way she had thought they were. Not her mother. Not nerdy Andrew. Not rotten Carter. Not her father.

Especially not her father.

I'm going to see him, she thought, suddenly quite sure about it. When I'm ready. Mom probably won't like it, but it's something I'm going to do. After all, I lied, too. I told him I'd go with him. But I couldn't. Not like that. But maybe someday . . .

What about right now, though? What about her? Was she still the old Spider? A new Spider? How could she tell? Lately, she'd felt big and small so many times it was scary. And yet . . . and yet it was as if a door stood open ahead of her now, just a crack. A door to somewhere she really wanted to be.

Spider thought about that. Then she shrugged. You never knew what might happen, really.

She went back inside and walked over to the computer. Picking up her baseball cap, she stood looking at it for a moment. Then she settled it on sideways, tweaking her ponytail out through the hole, and booted up the computer.

Colors swirled, and the Cat appeared, grinning. Andrew's dopey grin.

"Hey, widget-brain," she said, grinning back.

"That doesn't compute," it replied. "But I get the general drift. Anyway, what's your pleasure?"

"Zap me to the Net, beast," said Spider.

"Yo," said the Cat.

And did.

About the Author

Sharon Stewart was born in Kamloops, British Columbia. After pursuing a successful academic career as a history teacher, she turned her sights toward the writing life, a childhood ambition that reemerged as she began editing for educational publishers. She has worked as an editor and writer for fifteen years now, and her stories and poems have appeared in many anthologies. *Spider's Web* is Sharon Stewart's third novel for young adults. It was initially inspired by her own experiences on the Net (though she has never *flamed* anyone!) and by an article she read on Bill Gates' wired mansion. As she continued to research the Net, Sharon Stewart became fascinated with the idea that people can become anyone they want online. Once that possibility became part of her story, it didn't take long for *Spider's Web* to evolve into a humorous, fast-paced, technological adventure.

PHOTO BY ECLIPSE PHOTOGRAPHY